Adam crushed the [...] it into the bottom of his [...] against the wall of a nearby locker—stupid idea, since all it produced was a dull thud and a sharp pain, neither of which went very far toward alleviating his frustration.

But a stupid idea seemed appropriate; after all, what other kind did he have?

Fifty-eight percent.

Maybe if he and Miranda had spent more time working and less time playing video games and talking about Harper . . . At the time, it had seemed like the right thing to do. For those few hours, he'd felt more normal and more hopeful than he had in a long time.

She was a good friend, he'd realized.

Just maybe not a very good tutor.

Or maybe it's just me, Adam thought in disgust. He'd actually studied this time, staring at the equations long enough that at least a few of them should have started to make sense and weld themselves to his brain.

Fifty-eight percent. It was scrawled in an angry red, next to a big, circled **F** and a note reading *Come see me.*

Instead, Adam dumped his stuff in his locker and walked out of school, the pounding of his footsteps mirrored by the rhythmic battering of a single word against his brain:

Stupid.

Stupid.

Stupid.

SEVEN DEADLY SINS

Lust
Envy
Pride
Wrath
Sloth

SOON TO BE COMMITTED:
Gluttony

SEVEN DEADLY SINS

Sloth

ROBIN WASSERMAN

SIMON PULSE

New York   London   Toronto   Sydney

This book is a work of fiction. Any references to historical events, real people, or real locales are used fictitiously. Other names, characters, places, and incidents are the product of the author's imagination, and any resemblance to actual events or locales or persons, living or dead, is entirely coincidental.

SIMON PULSE
An imprint of Simon & Schuster Children's Publishing Division
1230 Avenue of the Americas, New York, NY 10020
Copyright © 2006 by Robin Wasserman
All rights reserved, including the right of reproduction in whole or in part in any form.
SIMON PULSE and colophon are registered trademarks of Simon & Schuster, Inc.
Designed by Ann Zeak
The text of this book was set in Bembo.
Manufactured in the United States of America
First Simon Pulse edition December 2006
10 9 8 7 6 5 4 3 2 1
Library of Congress Control Number 2005937176
ISBN-13: 978-1-4169-0718-3
ISBN-10: 1-4169-0718-1

For Aunt Sherry and Uncle Jim,
and for Brandon,
who likes to sleep

How heavy do I journey on the way
When what I seek, my weary travel's end,
Doth teach that ease and that repose to say,
"Thus far the miles are measured from thy friend."
—William Shakespeare, "Sonnet 50"

Nothing to do
Nowhere to go
I wanna be sedated
—The Ramones, "I Wanna Be Sedated"

c h a p t e r

1

"I'm in heaven," Harper moaned as the masseur kneaded his supple fingers into the small of her back. "You were right, this is exactly what we needed."

Kaia shooed away her own masseur and turned over onto her back, almost purring with pleasure as the sun warmed her face. "I'm always right."

"I wouldn't go that far," Harper snarked, but there was no venom in her tone. The afternoon sun had leached away most of her will to wound—and a half hour under Henri's magic fingers had taken care of the rest. "Mmmmm, could life get any better?"

"Zhoo are steel verreee tense," Henri told her in his heavy French accent.

"And zhoo are steel verreee sexeeeee," Kaia murmured, in an impeccable accent of her own. The girls exchanged a glance as the hunky but clueless Henri smoothed a palmful of warm lotion across Harper's back.

"This weeel help you reeelax," he assured her. As if

anyone could relax with a voice like that purring in her ear. "I leave you ladies now. *Au revoir, mes chéries.*"

"*Arrivederci,* Henri!" Harper cried, giggling at the rhyme.

"That's Italian," Kaia sneered. "Idiot."

"Who cares?" Harper countered. "Snob."

"Loser."

"Bitch." Harper narrowly held back a grin.

"Slut." Kaia's eyes twinkled.

"Damn right!" Harper pulled herself upright and raised her mojito in the air. Kaia did the same, and they clinked the plastic cocktail glasses together. "To us. Good thing we found each other—"

"—since no one else could stand us," Kaia finished, and they burst into laughter.

It was the kind of day where the clouds look painted onto the sky. The scene was straight out of a travel brochure—five star all the way, of course. Storybook blue sky, turquoise ocean lapping away at the nearby shore, gleaming white sand beach, and a warm tropical breeze rustling through their hair, carrying the distant strains of a reggae band. The girls stretched out along on their deck chairs, their every need attended to by a flotilla of servants.

"I could stay here forever." Harper sighed. She let her leg slip off the chair and dug her bare toe into the sand, burrowing it deeper and deeper into the cool, dark ground. "I wish we never had to go back."

"I don't know about you," Kaia drawled, "but I don't *have* to do anything."

"Right," Harper snorted. "The great and powerful Kaia Sellers, with the world at her fingertips. As if you can ditch real life and just stay here in paradise."

"I can do anything I want. Haven't you figured that out yet?"

Harper rolled her eyes.

"Why not?" Kaia continued. "What do I have to go back for? What do you? Isn't that why we came out here in the first place, to leave all that shit behind?"

Harper sighed. "You're right. And it worked. I can barely even remember what we were escaping from, and—" Her eyes widened. "You're bleeding." A small trail of blood trickled down Kaia's temple; Harper raised her hand to her own face, as if expecting to feel a similar wound.

Kaia frowned for a moment, dabbing her head with a napkin. "Just a mosquito bite," she said with a shrug. She took a closer look at Harper, whose face had gone pale. "You were totally freaked, weren't you?"

"No," Harper lied. "It's just gross. All these bugs . . ." She swatted at a mosquito that had just landed on her bare leg, then another whizzing past her nose. "They're everywhere."

"Easy way to fix that." Kaia stood up, her bronze Dolce bikini blending seamlessly into her deep tan. "Come on." Without waiting to see if her orders were followed—after all, they always were—she bounded toward the shoreline, kicking up a spray of sand in her wake.

Harper raced after her, and they reached the ocean's edge at the same moment. Harper stopped short as a wave of icy water splashed against her ankles, but Kaia didn't even hesitate. She waded out, the water rising above her calves, her knees, her thighs, and then, submerged to her waist, she turned and flashed Harper a smile. It was the eager, mischievous grin of a little kid sneaking into the deep end even though she's not quite sure how to swim.

3

Harper waved, frozen in place, unable to force herself to go any deeper into the churning water, unwilling to go back.

Kaia took a deep breath, closed her eyes, and dove under the surface, her arms slicing through the water, pulling her into the deep. She resurfaced, gasping for air, and leaned back into an easy float, the salt water buoying her body, the gentle waves bouncing her up and down. Harper's shouts, dim and incoherent, blew past with the wind, but Kaia dipped her head back and the roaring water in her ears drowned out the noise.

Harper stood in the same spot, the tide carving deep rivulets around her feet as the waves washed in and back out again. The wind picked up, but the sky remained clear and blue. Harper stood, and Harper watched, and Kaia floated farther and farther out to sea—

And then she woke up.

She'd hoped the dreams would stop once she weaned herself off the Percodan. They hadn't. Just like the phantom pains that still tore through her legs when she tried to sleep, they'd outstayed their welcome.

For a long time, the pain had kept her awake.

Ambien had helped with that, the little pink pills that carried her mind away. But when sleep came, so did the dreams. They weren't always nightmares. Sometimes they were nice, carrying her away to somewhere warm and safe. Those were the worst. Because always, in the end, she woke up.

It was better just not to sleep.

But she needed her strength, they were always telling her. *For what?* she wanted to ask. For tolerating her disgustingly bubbly physical therapist? For avoiding phone calls and turning away visitors? For limping from her bedroom to the kitchen and back again? For zoning out through a *Little House on the Prairie* marathon because she was too lazy to change the channel? For turning two weeks of recuperation into four, inventing excuse after excuse until she no longer knew how much of the pain was real and how much was just expedient?

Maybe they were right. Because her strength had finally given out. She'd run out of imagined excuses, and the big day had arrived: back to school.

She'd already picked out the perfect outfit: an eggplant-colored peasant top with a tight bodice and sufficiently low neckline, a tan ruffled skirt that flared out at the bottom, and, just for added panache, a thin, gauzy black scarf woven through with sparkly silver.

After a long, too hot shower she slipped into the outfit, certain it made the right statement: *I'm back.* She brushed out her hair and mechanically applied her eye shadow, mascara, a touch of gloss, barely looking in the mirror; it was as if she went through the routine every morning, and this weren't the first time she'd dispensed with her cozy gray sweats since—

Since the accident. Since what had happened.

It still hurt her to say the words. It hurt to think them. And that was unacceptable. She couldn't afford to indulge in that kind of frailty, especially not today, when everyone would surely be staring at her, the walking wounded, waiting for a sign of weakness.

So she'd been practicing. Every day, she forced herself to think the unthinkable, to speak the hateful words aloud. She whispered them to herself before she drifted off to sleep, in hopes of forestalling the dreams. She murmured them while watching TV, while waiting for the doctor, while pushing her untouched food around on the plate— she had once shouted them at top volume, her stereo turned up loud enough to drown out her voice.

Speaking the truth didn't make it seem any more real. In fact, it sounded just as strange, just as surreal, each time it trickled off her tongue. And it always hurt. But she was hurting *herself*, and that gave her power. It made her feel strong, reminding her that there was nothing left to be afraid of.

She said them to herself now, as she hovered in the doorway, gathering her strength to face the day. The first day. She ran a hand through her hair, willing it not to shake. She zipped up the new boots that rose just high enough to cover the bandage on her left calf. She applied a final layer of Tarte gloss, then practiced her smile. It had to look perfect. Everything had to look perfect.

She took a deep breath and held herself very still. And then, softly but firmly, she said it:

"Kaia is dead."

And with that, Harper Grace was ready to go.

✧✧✧

"Haven High!
Haven High!
Haven High!"

Beth Manning did her best to hold back a sigh at the roars of the crowd. When she'd volunteered to organize Senior Spirit Week, she hadn't taken into account the fact that it would require so much . . . spirit. That meant mustering up some kind of enthusiasm for the place she was most desperate to leave.

But that was her penance, right?

She forced herself to smile as she handed out the carefully crafted info packets to the rest of the Senior Spirit team. Too many tasks and not enough people meant Beth had been up for two days straight pulling things together; despite a morning espresso and a late-morning Red Bull, her energy level was still in the toilet.

"Let's hear it for the senior class!" she shouted now into the microphone, tossing back her long blond hair and aiming a blazing smile out at the crowd. She pumped her fist in the air, trying to ignore the embarrassment creeping over her. So she sounded like a cheerleader. So what? "Are you ready for an awesome end to an awesome year?" she cried.

College apps were in. Decisions were pending. Grades were irrelevant. And, as tradition dictated, the senior class was treated to a whirlwind of activity: a senior auction, a community service day, a school spirit day, student-teacher sports challenges—day after day of celebration, kicked off by this inane afternoon rally. An official Haven High welcome to the beginning of the end, capped off by a very unofficial blow-out party.

There'd be a lot of hangovers in the next couple weeks.

And a lot of girls weeping and guys manfully slapping one another on the back as the realization began to sink in: High school came with an expiration date.

It couldn't arrive soon enough, Beth thought, as she announced the schedule of upcoming activities in the perkiest voice she could muster.

Once, she would have enjoyed all of this. Even the marching band's off-key rendition of the school song. Even the cheerleaders firing up the crowd and the jocks preening under the spotlight. Especially the jocks—one of them in particular. Beth had been eager for college; she'd spent half her life preparing—studying, working, saving, dreaming—but she hadn't been eager to leave behind everything and everyone she knew. She would have mourned and celebrated with the rest of them, cheered and shouted and wept and hugged until it was all over.

But that was before.

As she stepped away from the microphone to let the student council president make his speech, Beth's gaze skimmed across the crowd—until, without meaning to, she locked eyes with Harper. Only for a second. Then a lock of curly auburn hair fell across Harper's face, hiding it from view, and Beth looked away.

One glance had been enough to confirm it: The queen was back. Her lady-in-waiting Miranda hovered dutifully by her side, and in the row behind them, fallen courtier Adam, angling to get back into his lady's good graces. It was as if nothing had ever happened, and from the self-assured smile on Harper's face, Beth could tell that was just the way she liked it. Surely it would only be a matter of time before Harper and Adam picked up where they left off—

Stop, she reminded herself. She was done with all that bitterness, anger, and—she could admit it now—jealousy. She was better than that. And she owed Harper the bene-fit of the doubt, even if her former rival could never know why. She owed everyone the benefit of the doubt; that's what she had decided on that day last month. When

SLOTH

you've screwed up everything, not just stepped over but set fire to the line, you needed all the good karma you could get. When you can't apologize for what you've done, and you can't fix it, all you can do is forgive others, and try to make everything better. And Beth was trying, starting with herself.

Even when it was hard; even when it seemed impossible.

After the accident, things are strange for days. Silent, still, as if a loud voice could break through the fragile frame of reality that they were slowly trying to rebuild. Eyes are rimmed with red, hands tremble, empty spaces sprinkle the classroom—absent faces who couldn't bear to stare at the chair that will stay empty forever.

Beth wants to stare at the chair in French class, but she sits in the front. So all she can do is tune out the substitute and imagine it behind her. And in her imagination, the seat is filled.

I'm not responsible, *Beth tells herself. It has become her* mantra. Not my fault. Not my fault.

But that feels like a lie. A comforting lie, supported by cool logic and endless rationales, but a lie nonetheless. There are too many what-ifs. What if Harper had been in the school, rather than in the car? What if Kaia had gone inside, rather than drive away? What if Harper hadn't had such a reason to escape?

Step one to being a better person: Forgive. She sees Adam every day at her locker, and on the fourth day, she talks to him.

"I'm not angry anymore," she says, wishing that it were true. "I don't hate you. Life's too short."

And it is. But when she looks at him, all she can think about is his bare body on top of Kaia's, the things they must have done together. And when he beams and hugs her, she can't forget that he pledged his love, then betrayed her. He slept with Kaia. She can't forgive that, not really.

Of course, she forgives Kaia, she reminds herself. Of course. Next up is Kane.

"*Apology accepted*," *she says, although he never apologized. He wrecked her life—tricked Adam into dumping her, fooled her into turning to Kane for comfort, trashing her reputation when the truth came out—and he walked away unscathed. Kaia helped. Not because there was anything in it for her; just for the fun of it. Just to see what would happen.*

"*I hope we can be friends*," *Beth says, hoping she never has to speak to him again.*

Kane nods and walks away. He knows a lie when he sees it.

Beth smiles as she closes her locker. She smiles as she waves at someone across the hall.

She should start smiling more, she decides. Being a better person is supposed to feel good; she should look the part.

A round of applause snapped Beth back to the present, and she realized it was time to step up to the mic and wrap things up. "Welcome to senior spring," she announced, her voice nearly lost amid the cheers. "Let's get ready for the best time of our lives!"

"Is everything okay?" Miranda asked again.

Harper nodded, shifting her position on the narrow metal bench. The bleachers couldn't be very comfortable for her, Miranda suddenly realized, feeling like an idiot. Her leg was still healing, and with a sore neck and back . . .

"Do you want to take off?" Miranda asked. "We don't have to stay if you don't—"

"I'm fine," Harper said quietly. She stared straight ahead, as if mesmerized by Beth's ridiculous speech. A few months ago, the two of them would have been soaking up every absurd word, adding ammunition to their anti-Beth arsenal. Later Miranda would have them both cracking up over her Beth impersonation, complete with bright smile and frequent hair toss.

Or more likely, they would have skipped the rally altogether, snuck off campus to gossip and complain, then drunk a toast to their high school days drawing to a party-filled close.

Instead, Harper had insisted on attending. It was her first day back, and maybe she'd been looking forward to the crowds and excitement, or maybe she'd just wanted to get it over with; Miranda didn't know. She hadn't asked.

"Do you need anything?" she asked instead. "I could get us something to drink, or—"

"No. I'm fine."

"Are you sure?"

"Miranda, I'm *fine*," Harper snapped. "Can you give it a rest?"

"I'm sorry, I—"

"No, I'm sorry." Harper shifted in her seat again, rubbing her lower back. Miranda successfully resisted the urge to comment. "Really." Harper smiled—and maybe someone who hadn't been her best friend for almost a decade would have bought it. "I'm just ... can we talk about something else? Please." It wasn't a request. It was an order.

No problem; Miranda was used to talking about something else. It's all they'd been doing since that first day, when Harper had finally agreed to visitors. Miranda had been on her best behavior; and she'd stayed that way.

Among the questions she knew better than to ask:

How do you feel?

What's it like?

Do you miss her?

What were you on, and why, when you humiliated yourself in front of the whole school?

Why did you get into the car? Where were you going?

What really happened?

It had been a long month of unspoken rules, and Miranda was almost grateful for them, as if they were bright flags dotting a minefield, warning her where not to step.

They never spoke Kaia's name.

They never talked about the fight, the betrayal that Miranda had forgiven the moment her phone rang with the news.

It made things easier. Like now—Miranda knew better than to mention the last time she'd been in this auditorium, shivering in an upper row of the bleachers while student after student somberly spoke of Kaia's grace and fortitude. Her beauty, her wit, her style—they never mentioned her cruelty or her penchant for causing misery, the way she thrived on other people's pain. They never mentioned the rumors swirling around her relationship with a certain former French teacher, lying in a hospital bed of his own, Kaia's fingerprints found at the scene of the apparent crime.

A wreath of flowers had lain at the center of the court, right where the Haven High mascot was currently doing cartwheels to rally the crowd. An enormous photograph of Kaia, bundled up in cashmere with windblown hair and rosy cheeks, had stood behind the podium, where Beth now raised her hands and clasped them in triumph. Kaia's father had already left town, maybe for good; Harper was still in the hospital. Miranda had sat alone, trying to force her mind to appreciate the tragedy of wasted youth, to force herself to weep or shake like all those girls who'd never even spoken to Kaia, who knew her only as the newish girl with the Marc Jacobs bag—unlike Miranda, who'd shared drinks with Kaia, shared a limo with Kaia, shared a best friend with Kaia.

Kaia, who was now dead.

That should mean something. It should be a turning point, one of those moments that make you see the world in a new way.

But everything had seemed pretty much the same to Miranda, except that now the second-tier girls had a new strategy for sneaking onto the A-list; they'd been unable to befriend Kaia in life, but now there was nothing to stop them. It was still the same game, and it didn't interest her.

She'd thought instead about Harper, who, she'd been told, was in stable condition and recovering well. No visitors allowed, patient's orders.

She'd thought about how strange it was to see her math teacher cry.

She'd thought about whether her chem test that day would be cancelled.

And that was about it.

"So I've decided I hate all my clothes," Miranda said now, plucking at her pale blue T-shirt that had been washed so many times, she could no longer tell when it was inside out. "We're talking serious fashion emergency—and you know what that means. . . ."

Harper didn't say anything.

"Shopping spree," Miranda chirped. "You, me, Grace's

finest clothing stores, and, of course"—she patted her purse—"mom's gold card."

A faint smile crept across Harper's face. "I could use some new . . ."

"Everything?" Miranda prompted.

"You know it." She rolled her eyes. "Not that anything in this town would be worth buying—you know Grace."

"It's a total fashion—" Miranda cut herself off just in time. *Train wreck,* she'd been about to say. "Wreck" was too close to "collision." Accident. And that was another thing on the list of what they couldn't discuss. "Wasteland," she said instead. "I guess if you want, we could drive down Route 53 and pick up some swank duds at Wal-Mart. . . ."

Harper laughed, and it actually sounded real. "I'll pass, thanks. Hopefully Classic Rags will have some good stuff, and we can check out—oh."

"What?"

"It's nothing." Harper glanced off to the side. "It's just, I'm supposed to go to physical therapy this afternoon . . . but it's totally stupid. I can just blow it off."

"No!"

Harper's eyes widened, and Miranda softened her tone. "I just mean, no, you should go. We can shop anytime. You have to take care of yourself."

"It's really no big deal," Harper argued. Her fingers tightened around the edge of the bleacher seat.

"But you really should—"

"I guess, maybe. . . ."

"Unless there's some reason you actually want to—"

"Forget it." Harper stood up, wincing a bit as she put

weight on her left leg. "You're right, we can shop another time. I'll see you later, okay?"

"Where are you going?" Miranda jumped up from her seat. "I'll come with you."

"I've got some stuff to do," Harper said, already walking away. "You should stick around here."

Once again, it wasn't a request. It was an order.

"Where are you taking me?" the redhead giggled as Kane Geary led her, blindfolded, down the empty hallway.

"That's for me to know"—he kissed the back of her neck, then ran his fingers lightly down her spine, relishing the burst of shivers it caused—"and you to find out. Come on"—Sarah? Stella? Susan?—"babe. Time to make your dreams come true."

He pulled her along faster, but she tugged back, slowing them down. "I can't see anything," she reminded him, squeezing his hand. "I'm going to trip."

"I'd never let you fall," he assured her. "Don't you trust me?"

She laughed. "I'm not that stupid."

Kane begged to differ. But not out loud.

"How about you take off the blindfold and just tell me where you're taking me?"

"Where's the fun in that?" Kane shook his head. "I've got a better idea." He hoisted her over his shoulder. Once she stopped wriggling and giggling, she lay pressed against him, her arms wrapped around his waist and her lips nuzzling the small of his back.

"All the blood's rushing to my head, Kane," she complained, "so you'd better hurry."

But he stopped.

A month ago, Kaia's locker had been transformed into a makeshift shrine, with a rainbow of cards and angel pictures adorning the front, above an ever-growing pile of flowers and teddy bears. There were notes, bracelets, magazine cutouts, candles—an endless supply of sentimental crap—but no photos. None of the mourners had any pictures of Kaia; none of them even knew her.

Even Kane had no pictures. Back in the fall, he, Kaia, and Harper had staged an illicit photo shoot, a faux hookup between Harper and Kane captured on film—and later doctored to make it appear that Beth was the one in his arms. Kane still had the original images stored away for a rainy day; but Kaia had stayed behind the lens. And Kane's mental picture was blurry. He remembered the way she'd felt, the one night they spent together—he remembered her lips, her skin, her sighs. But the room had been dark, and she'd been gone by morning.

For the first few days, there had been a strange zone of silence around her locker—you dropped your voice when you passed by, or you avoided it altogether. But then it faded into the background, just one of those things you barely noticed as you hurried down the hall.

Even Kane, who noticed everything, had successfully blocked it out after a few days of cringing and sneering. He'd almost forgotten it was there.

And now it really wasn't.

The collage of cards and pictures had disappeared, with only a few stray, peeling strips of tape to remember them by. The pile of junk was gone—only a single teddy bear and a couple of votive candles remained, and as Kane watched, they too were swept up by the janitor, deposited in a large bin, and wheeled away.

Now it was just any other locker. Reduce, reuse, recycle.

"Kane, what is it?" the redhead asked, tickling his side. "Are we here? Wherever we are?"

"No, we're not here," he said, still staring at the locker. "We're nowhere."

It's just a locker, he told himself. *She doesn't need it anymore.*

He put the redhead back on her feet, tipped her blind-folded head toward his, and gave her a long kiss. Then he put his arm around her shoulder and guided her away from the locker, down the hall, toward the empty boiler room, where he'd prepared his standard romantic spread.

"We're two of a kind," Kaia had once told him. Meaning: icy, detached, heartless. Winners, who didn't need anyone else's approval to be happy, who sought out what they wanted and took it. Who didn't look back.

Wouldn't it be a fitting tribute to prove her right?

2

Adam was waiting on his front stoop when the car pulled into the driveway.

At first, he didn't move, just watched as Mrs. Grace climbed out of the rusty Volvo, then scurried around to the passenger's side to help her daughter.

Harper shrugged her off.

If you didn't know her, she would have looked perfectly normal, Adam mused. Aside from a few fading scratches on her face and neck, and a long scar on her left arm, she looked totally fine. The same. And from a distance, you couldn't even see that much; he'd only noticed the scar this afternoon at the rally, sitting behind her, close enough to see the thin white line arcing across her unusually pale skin, close enough for her to see him—and turn away.

From this distance, all he could see was her wild hair curling around her face, and the syncopated rhythm of her walk—not the familiar stride of superiority, as if she were a wealthy landowner touring her property, but a more tentative, irregular gait, small nervous steps that favored her right leg.

He called out; she didn't stop. But she was moving slowly enough that he could catch her.

"Adam, what a pleasant surprise," Amanda Grace said, favoring him with her unintentionally condescending smile—at least, he'd always assumed it was unintentional. Amanda Grace had always been nothing but kind to the boy next door, and probably had no idea how obvious her disdain for his mother or his circumstances truly was.

By any objective standard, her family was worse off than his—after all, his mother was the top Realtor in town, while the Graces ran a dry cleaners that even in good years barely broke even. But Adam and his trailer park refugee mother had poor white trash written all over them—and his mother's not-so-circumspect bed-hopping didn't help matters—while the Graces had their name.

It was pretty much all they had, aside from the stately but dilapidated home left over from boom times, but in the town of Grace, California, surrounded by Grace Library, Grace Hospital, Grace Retirement Village, their name was enough.

"Would you like to come inside, Adam?" she asked, putting a hand on Harper's shoulder; Harper squirmed away. "I'm sure you could use a home-cooked meal."

"I'm sure he's got other plans," Harper said, her glare making it clear to Adam that if he didn't, he'd better make some.

"In that case, I'll give you two a chance to talk. Don't stay out too long, hon," she cautioned Harper as she stepped inside the house. "You need your rest."

"I'm *fine*, Mother."

Adam tasted victory. He was sure Harper had been about to duck inside as well—but now that her mother had cautioned her, Adam knew she'd stay out as long as possible. Even if it meant talking to him.

"What do you want?" she asked, and again, if you didn't know her, you'd think her voice perfectly pleasant. But Adam knew her—had grown up with her, briefly dated her, been betrayed by her, was finished with her—or so he'd thought, until he realized what "finished" could mean.

"Just wanted to see how you're doing," he said. "You haven't been returning my phone calls, and this afternoon we . . . didn't get a chance to talk." Because she'd kept her back to him the whole time and had left as quickly as she could.

"How sweet," she said coolly. "Thank you for asking. I'm fine, as you can see. So . . . ?"

"So?" he repeated hopefully, after a long pause.

"*So* is there anything else?"

"Oh." Adam looked down at his scuffed sneakers. "I thought we could hang out," he suggested. "We could go get some coffee, or just, you know, go out back. On the rock."

On our *rock,* he wanted to say, the large, flat bed of granite that separated their two backyards, where they'd played G.I. Joes, shared their secrets, kissed under the moonlight.

"I'm not really in the rock-sitting mood," she told him.

"Then let's go out," he pressed. "There's some band playing at the Lost and Found, and—"

"What band?"

Was that honest curiosity in her voice?

"Something like Blind Rabbits. Or maybe Blind Apes? I don't know—it's just some guys from school, and I'm sure they suck, but—"

"What do you want from me, Adam?" The curiosity—and all other emotion—was gone from her face. And in its blankness, it looked familiar. It looked like Kaia.

"Nothing. Just—I thought we could have some fun together. I want . . ." Screw the casual act, he decided. Nothing between them had ever been casual, and she couldn't change that just by pretending they were strangers. "I want to be there for you, Gracie." She flinched at the sound of her old nickname, but her face stayed blank. "I want to be your friend."

"You can't always get what you want," she half said, half sang, in a tuneless rendition of the Rolling Stones lyric. "And I'm not granting wishes these days. Sorry."

"I'm sorry too."

He has never seen her look so small, or so pale. She is swaddled in white sheets, her bandaged arms exposed and lying flat at her sides. He tries to ignore the tubes and wires, the intimidating machines with their flashing lights and insistent beeping.

Her eyes are closed. She's only sleeping, he tells himself.

But it's difficult to believe that when she's so pale and still.

The last time he spoke to her, he told her she was worthless—that he would be better off without her in his life. Everyone would be better off, he'd suggested. She told him she loved him. And he told her it wasn't love—it couldn't be, because she didn't have that in her. He'd sent her away.

And then she'd appeared onstage, drugged out and miserable, begging him to take her back in front of the whole school.

He'd been humiliated. Enraged. Until he got the phone call.

He sits down on the small plastic folding chair next to her bed and cradles her hand in his, careful not to move her arm. He doesn't want to hurt her. She doesn't wake up.

The room is empty. Her parents are in the cafeteria. The nurse just left. Adam is alone, and he can say what he needs to say. Even if she can't hear him.

"Please be okay," he begs her. "I need you."

He wishes she would open her eyes. Or squeeze his hand.

Talk to her, they'd told him. It can help.

"Remember when we were in fourth grade and I forgot my permission slip for that trip to the amusement park?" he asks. He feels stupid, even though there's no one to hear. But he keeps going. "And I started crying in front of everyone when Mrs. Webber told me I couldn't go? You tore your permission slip in half so you'd have to stay there with me. You missed out on your first roller coaster—" He stops and closes his eyes. He doesn't want to remember. "Just for me," he whispers. He wants to lay his head on her chest and listen to her heartbeat, confirm that it's steady and strong. But there are too many bandages and wires, and he's afraid he could hurt her. Even more.

He leans down, his face close to hers, and for a moment he is tempted to kiss her, convinced that, like Sleeping Beauty, the touch of his lips might bring her back. Instead, he rests his head on the pillow next to hers and whispers. He asks her to wake up. He tells her, again, that he needs her.

Still, she sleeps.

Adam lies motionless for a moment, watching her breathe, soothed by the rhythmic rise and fall of the white sheets. Then he sits up, stands, and says good-bye.

"I've got to go," he says. "I'm sorry. But I'll be back tomorrow."

If he had forgiven her sooner, and she hadn't made that speech . . .

If he had caught her before she had run out of the building . . .

If he had followed her to the parking lot, stopped her from getting into the car . . .

He knows she can't hear him, but he says it again. "I'm sorry."

"Nothing to be sorry about," Harper said, and the artificially casual tone was back in her voice. "I've got all the friends I need right now, and like I say, I'm fine, so you can forget that whole guilty conscience thing."

"That's not—"

"Better get inside now," she said, staring at a point over his shoulder. "Or my mother will send the dogs out for me. Thanks for stopping by."

"Harper, if we could just—"

"See you around." She turned her back on him and walked inside the house.

Adam wasn't ready to go home. No one was waiting for him there. So he circled around the back of his house and hoisted himself up onto their rock. He could see Harper's bedroom window; the shades were drawn. He lay back against the cool granite, staring up at the hazy sky, tinged with a grayish purple.

He thought he should be angry, or sorry, or hopeless. But he was just tired. He closed his eyes, and waited for sleep.

"Dude, get up!"

"Whuh . . . ?" Reed Sawyer propped himself up and shook his head, trying to get his bearings. A thick fog hung over his brain, courtesy of a mid-afternoon toke and nap session. But gradually, the blur of noise and color resolved itself into comprehensible details, and the world clicked back into place.

The cold, hard metal beneath him—the hood of his bandmate's car.

The loud voice harshing his buzz, the heavy hand shaking him awake—said bandmate.

The big emergency—a gig, their first in weeks. Tonight. Now.

Reed nodded to himself as the facts crawled back into his brain. He lay back against the hood and pulled out another joint. His fingers fumbled with the lighter, but it lit up, and a moment later, so did he.

He sucked in and grinned. That first lungful was his favorite part, the sweet familiar burn spreading through his body. Peace.

"What's with you—get the hell up!" The hand was shaking him again. His eyes had slipped closed without him noticing. Things were easier in the dark.

"Chill, Fish," he groaned. "I'm up."

"The gear's packed up, we've got to go," Fish complained. "What's with you, man? Do you *want* to be late?"

Did he want to be late? Reed didn't want . . . anything. To want, you had to think about the future, you had to think outside the moment. Reed drew in another lungful of smoke. Thinking about the future only led you to the past; it was safer to stay in the present.

"I'm coming," he said, digging into the pocket of his jeans to make sure he had his lucky guitar pick. "In a minute."

"Right." Fish grabbed his arm and dragged him up. "Get your ass off my car. You're coming now." He rolled his eyes and, with a laugh, grabbed the joint out of Reed's hand. "Didn't your mother ever teach you to share?"

As they ambled toward the van, Fish babbled about the gig, about possibilities, new songs, recording, making it big. Pointless dreams, Reed realized that now. But he kept his mouth shut.

The band didn't seem to matter much to him these days. Nothing did. Not since—

Before it happened, he'd almost gotten himself kicked out of school. He'd refused to apologize for something he hadn't done. It had seemed so important then: upholding his honor. Telling the truth.

At the thought of it, Reed almost laughed. What the hell was the difference? That's what he'd figured out, after the accident. It didn't matter what you did or didn't do. If life wanted to kick you in the ass, no one could stop it. If the universe wanted to take away the one thing that mattered . . .

So he'd given in. He confessed, he took the suspension, went back to school. It was what everyone wanted, and that made it easy. He hadn't stopped to think about what he wanted. Because he didn't want anything. Not anymore.

"We got a surprise for you." Fish ran a hand through his greasy blond hair—he'd decided the tousled, windblown look would get him more girls. Stuck at the back of the stage, behind the drums, only his head was visible, he always pointed out. He couldn't do anything about his face, but the hair was a constant work in progress.

"Uh-huh."

"Aren't you curious?"

"No."

"You don't want a surprise?" Fish asked, sounding put out.

"Do I get a choice?"

Fish shrugged. "Good point." They'd reached the van, and Reed headed toward the driver's seat, as always. But Fish pushed him toward the back. "Not today. I'm driving, Hale has shotgun. You're in back."

Reed shook his head and slung himself into the van—nearly landing in the lap of a tall, skinny brunette who was sprawled along the length of the backseat. Her legs were nearly bare, along with the rest of her.

"Uh . . . Fish?"

"Surprise!" Hale chuckled and twisted around to face the backseat. "Reed, meet Sandra. We thought she could cheer you up. She's a *big* fan." Hale's hands flickered briefly at his chest, universal code for bigness of a certain shape and form. Reed didn't need the tip. Sandra was bulging out of a tight leather halter top, her breasts seeming ready to escape at any moment.

"The boys told me I could ride along with you," Sandra said, in a soft, flighty voice. "Hope you don't mind."

He didn't want to touch her; but she was lying across his seat and showed no sign of moving. He nudged her gently and squeezed himself in. She grabbed his hand. "I love guitarists," she said, massaging his fingers. "Such a strong grip, all that flexibility—"

"Let's get going," Reed said. He leaned against the dirty window and stared out at the dull scenery. He tried to ignore the pressure of Sandra's body leaning against his, and the way her fingers were playing up and down his thigh. The bar was close. They'd be there soon.

"Whatcha thinking about?" she asked, after a few minutes of silence.

"Nothing."

He wished it were true. But every time he tried to wipe his mind, the words came back. Her voice. It was his own fault—he'd listened to the voice mail, the last voice mail, so often that he'd memorized it. And even now, wishing he could forget it, he couldn't stop hearing her voice.

Reed, I don't know if you want to hear this, but I need to tell you that I'm sorry. I was wrong, about everything.

Then there was a pause, and a loud, deep breath.

I'm sure you don't want to talk to me, but—

Her voice shook on the word.

I need to talk to you, to explain. Just call me back. Please. Because I—

Another pause. And this one was the worst, because he would never know what Kaia was about to say. And because he knew the last two words would be the last, and she would never know if he accepted them.

I'm sorry.

The joint was burned out, and he lit another one.

"The strong, silent type," Sandra said, winding her finger through one of his curls. "I like." She edged closer.

He inhaled deeply, blew out a puff of smoke, and waited for the calm to settle over him again. There was no other escape.

The timing was suspicious. An hour after the Adam encounter and Miranda called, suggesting—*quel coincidence!*—a night out at the Lost and Found to see the Blind Monkeys.

Harper may have taken a hiatus from scheming, but she recognized the signs; so Miranda and Adam were teaming up to drag her out of the house and back to "normal" life? So be it. She had her own reasons for wanting to suffer through a Blind Monkeys performance; and if she ran into Adam, at least she'd be ready.

She just wasn't ready to face the *rest* of the senior class, Miranda having neglected to mention that the band was playing the official opening event for Senior Spirit Week. That meant crowds, noise, gossip, a night of public posturing . . . and no alcohol to dull the pain. At the request of Haven High, the Lost and Found had gone dry for the night, and Harper was left with few options. She and Miranda pulled two chairs up to a tiny, filthy table and set down their Cokes.

"This sucks," she complained, trying to make herself heard over the noise passing as music that was blasting out of a nearby speaker.

"What?" Miranda mouthed.

"This sucks!" Harper shouted. Miranda just shook her head, miming frustration. It was too loud for anything else. "I shouldn't have come," Harper said at normal volume, relishing the strange sensation of knowing no one would hear. "I hate—" She stopped, as the lyrics became clear.

Get out of my dreams.
Get out of my head.
Will I have to stick around this hell,
When I'm the one who's dead?

It was a shit song, but she knew who'd written it, and why. She'd wanted to see him—not *speak* to him, of course, but just watch him. Reed Sawyer, Kaia's . . . whatever. He was hunched over the mic, dark, shaggy hair falling across his glassy eyes, his voice coarse and throaty, scraping across the so-called melody.

She'd seen this band play once before, she suddenly realized. Months before, she'd come here with Adam, desperately hoping he would finally make his move, ending their friendship and starting something new. She'd come with Adam—but she'd left alone. And Adam had left with Kaia. Harper had cried and raged, while Kaia had whisked Adam away to an abandoned motel, laid him back on a sunken mattress, and fulfilled his fantasies.

Harper could still picture them together, in a dark recess of the bar, Kaia's hands in his hair, Kaia's tongue in his mouth. And the Blind Monkeys blasting in the background, shaking the floor as Harper stood perfectly still, trying not to scream.

That bitch, Harper thought, before she could stop herself. Then she felt sick. *I never should have come back here.*

"I have to get out of here," she told Miranda. But Miranda only looked at her quizzically and took another sip of her soda. "I HAVE TO GO!"

Miranda nodded and, totally misunderstanding, pointed off to the left, toward the bathrooms.

Harper already knew where they were. It's where Adam had gone that night. He'd stood up from their table, headed for the bathrooms—and had never come back.

Maybe he'd had the right idea.

She made it outside before realizing she had nowhere

to go. Miranda had the car keys, and it was too far to walk—especially when everything already felt so sore. Maybe it would be enough to stand outside, breathe some of that fresh air everyone always claimed was so helpful. She could wait it out. Maybe, eventually, she'd be able to go back inside.

Maybe not.

Harper leaned against the dank brick wall of the bar, not caring about the gunk that would surely rub off on her gauzy white shirt. Her leg hurt, her head hurt, and she needed some support. The wall would have to do.

"Who let you back out on the streets?" Kane smirked and leaned an arm against the wall, giving Harper a sardonic grin.

"What's it to you?"

"Just need to know who I should complain to," he teased. She rolled her eyes and turned away—he was sure it was to hide a smile. "Good to see you up and out, Grace."

"Miss me?" she asked, arching an eyebrow.

"I wouldn't say that—but you know I've got a low tolerance for boredom. And you definitely make things interesting."

"Gosh, I'm overwhelmed by your kindness and affection. Is this the part where you hug me and ask me how I'm doing?" Her tone was mocking, but Kane could tell she expected exactly that—and dreaded it.

Instead, he laughed. "You *have* been away for a long time," he said, shaking his head. "Why would I want to know how you're doing? I just want to know if you've got a cigarette."

That earned him his first real smile. And a pack of

Camel Reds. He pulled one out, tossed the pack back to her, and took his time lighting up. "So . . . ," he finally said. "Are we going in, or what?"

She waved lazily toward the entrance. "You go. Say hi to the pep squad for me. And enjoy your ginger ale."

"Meaning?"

"Meaning I'd rather bash my head into this wall than go back inside," she said bitterly. "But hey, be my guest."

"Better idea." He wiggled his eyebrows at her and cocked his head toward the parking lot. Translation: *Let's get out of here and get into some trouble.* "You in?"

"Let me just text Miranda," she said, whipping out her cell phone, "and then"—she did some rapid-fire number punching and flicked it shut again—"we're out of here."

She stumbled on the way to the car, and he caught her before she fell; but he resisted the urge to help her inside the silver Camaro. She was back on two feet again—she could do it herself. Or at least, he concluded, she thought she could. He slammed the door shut, started the car, slipped in his favorite CD and turned the pulsing rock beat up to top volume, and they were off.

Grace was a dead-end town whose residents led dead-end lives—meaning there were plenty of dark, dingy spots where you could drown your sorrows. And none of them carded.

They ended up nestled in a booth in the back of the Tavern, a nondescript bar and grill for the over-forty set, complete with a washed-out seventies decor and surly, middle-aged waitresses who'd been working there since the decorations were new.

Privacy guaranteed, or your money back.

Harper, after downing half a gin and tonic—her first in weeks—was already slurring her words. Kane, more on half-formed instinct than out of any reason or desire, had opted for root beer.

"When did you join AA?" Harper joked, flopping forward in her chair and propping her head in her hands. "Gonna leave me all alone to drown my sorrows?"

"Someone's got to drive you home," he pointed out as she downed the rest of her drink and waved the waitress over for another one.

"S'okay, I'm used to alone," she slurred, as if she hadn't heard him. "I mean, they're always there, *everyone's* always there, staring at me. Alone is good. They should all go away."

"You want me to stop staring at you?"

She let out a sharp bark of laughter, then slapped her hand over his. "Not you. You're the only one. You . . ." She stopped talking, distracted by the prospect of fishing the slice of lime out of the bottom of her glass.

"I . . . ?" he prodded.

"What? Oh. You don't give me that 'How are you doing' shit or 'Isn't it terrible aren't you traumatized what can I do' blah blah blah." She made a fake vomiting noise. "You don't care about what I do, you don't care about anyone but yourself. Thank God."

"Uh, thank you?" he asked sardonically. He leaned forward. This was the moment, he realized. Kane hated nothing more than not having the answers, and ever since that day in the hospital, he'd had nothing but questions. Her guard was down. She would answer. "Where'd you get the drugs, Grace?"

"Huh?"

"That day. The speech. What were you high on? And why?"

She shook her head furiously. "Not you, too!" But after a flicker of anger, she sighed loudly and slumped down in her chair. "Nothing," she said. "I told you. I told them. Nothing."

"Come on, Grace," he pushed. "They found them in your system. Everyone saw you up onstage—I heard what a head-case you were." *And I saw the way you pulled out of the parking lot. I saw the car skid out, I saw you drive away.* "You were on *something.*"

She shrugged her shoulders. "Believe me. Don't believe me. Who cares. And what's the difference? It's over now."

"Yeah, I guess. What's the difference?"

He is sitting in the waiting room, breathing shallowly. The scent of citrus-scented air freshener is overwhelming—but not enough to mask the smells beneath it. Old age, decay, vomit, blood, death. He hates hospitals. He hasn't been in one since he was a kid, sitting by his mother's bed, pretending not to know his father was crying out in the hall.

It's too soon, too fast, and no one knows everything, but as always, Kane knows enough. He has his sources.

One crash. Two girls, both thrown from the car. One with traces of psychotropic drugs in her bloodstream. One dead.

"Mr. Geary."

The cop sits down across from him. It's a woman, which he's not expecting. She's short and stocky in a dark gray blazer, her hair pulled back in a tight bun. Right out of central casting, he thinks. Not a coincidence—she probably takes her cues from Law & Order.

The thought depresses him.

"I'm told that you have some information that can be of assistance to us, Mr. Geary."

She has a sexy voice.

He shrugs. "I saw them leave the school," he says.

"Can you describe what you saw?" She doesn't ask what he was doing loitering on the back steps when the rest of the school was stuffed into the auditorium for a mandatory assembly.

"Harper ran out of the school."

"How did she appear?"

"What do you mean?" He knows. But he's not in the mood to help.

"Did she seem upset? Disoriented? Ineb—"

"She seemed in a hurry. She didn't stop to talk. She ran down to the parking lot. Kaia was standing there, by her car."

"What was she doing?"

The question hadn't occurred to Kane before. He didn't know the answer. He never would. "Standing. Staring. They talked for a while. Then they got into the car and drove away."

"Who was driving?"

It is the question he has been waiting for. She asks it casually, as if uninterested in the answer. He responds the same way, without pause, without hesitation, without thinking of Harper grabbing the keys, jumping inside, and tearing out of the lot.

"Kaia," he says with certainty. "It was her father's Beamer. She always drove."

They believe him. The evidence has all burned away. There's only his word. And when Harper wakes up, groggy and confused, she believes him too.

"I can't remember," she says, her voice soft but angry. These days, she is always angry. "Nothing. Just school, that morning, then . . . here. I can't remember." She closes her eyes and knits her *brow. She can't rub her forehead—her arms are caught in a web of wires and tubes. He surprises himself, pressing his palm to her head, brushing her hair off her face.*

"There's nothing to remember," he tells her. "You two got into the car. And Kaia drove away."

It's the last time he sees her. Soon she's done with visitors, except Miranda. But he knows she believes him.

They all do.

Some days, he even believes himself.

He drove Harper home, stopping only once for her to hop out and throw up in some bushes.

"Sorry," she said weakly, climbing back into the car.

"We've all been there," he assured her. "Just as long as you don't hurl in my car." He patted the dashboard fondly. "Then I dump you out on the side of the road and you can find your own way home."

She chuckled—then moaned and leaned forward, cradling her head in her arms as if the laughter made her brain hurt. He knew the feeling. "That's what I love about you," she said in a muffled voice. "There's no confusion about where your loyalties lie. You look out for your car—"

"Of course."

"You look out for yourself—"

"Naturally."

"And the rest of us can find our own way home."

"You know me too well, Grace." His fingers tightened around the steering wheel. "You always have."

chapter

3

"Can I carry your books for you?"

"Can I get you a soda?"

"Could I stand in line and get you some lunch?"

"She said *I* could stand in line!"

"But you got to drop her stuff at her locker—"

"Girls!" Harper massaged her temples as the two girls abruptly stopped their bickering.

"What is it?"

"What do you need?"

She sighed. She'd been waiting for this moment for three years, ever since she'd spent one eternal day sophomore year traipsing around after a bitchy blond senior with an undeserved superiority complex. King and Queen for a Day was a senior tradition—on paper, it meant that each underclassmen showered his or her designated senior with affection and treats. In reality, it meant spending the day being primped and pampered by your own personal servant—or, in Harper's case, two.

Who knew being waited on hand and foot could be so exhausting?

Of course, perhaps she could have enjoyed the novelty of the experience a bit more had the two underclassmen in question not spent the better part of the year following her around and imitating her every move. A theme song from one of those old Nick at Nite shows floated into her head: *"They laugh alike, they walk alike, at times they even talk alike—you can lose your mind . . ."*

That sounded about right. And now Mini-Me and her best friend Mini-She were stuck to her like glue, jockeying for the right to clean off her cafeteria seat. *The best time of my life?* Harper thought dryly. *Starting when?*

"Why don't you go get me something from the vending machine," she suggested to Mini-She, then turned to Mini-Me. "And you can go buy me some lunch."

"Coke? Diet Coke? Sprite? Vitamin Water? Gatorade? Snapple?"

"Salad? Meat loaf? Meat loaf and salad? And what kind of dressing? And what if there are fries? Or some kind of vegetable? Or—?"

"Vitamin water. Salad, make sure it's not just lettuce, Italian dressing. And—" It was going to be a long day; she deserved a treat. "Plenty of fries."

They were gone, and she was left with a blessed silence, so sweet that she was disinclined to scope out the cafeteria and find herself an appropriately high-powered table; better just to stand to the side for a moment and try to gather her strength. She'd been working on her icy, expressionless face, and she deployed it now. You never knew who was watching.

She didn't notice him at first—people like that flew below her radar; and even when she registered his presence, dimly, all she noticed were the ripped jeans and the scuffed sneakers, the long hair and the grease-stained fingers, and she expected him to pass her by.

It wasn't until he spoke that she looked at his face.

"Hey." He slouched against a wall and tilted his head down, looking up at her briefly, then looking away again, as if stealing glances at the sun.

"Hey." No stolen glances here; she stared, unabashedly, trying to figure out what Kaia had seen in him. There must have been something, but it was well disguised. True, his black T-shirt hugged some impressive arm muscles, and he did have that whole dark, sullen man of mystery thing going for him. But judging from the smell, the only mystery was how he'd managed to afford so much pot.

Probably grew his own, Harper decided. That's what they always did on TV.

She knew she should say something caustic and send him away; he wasn't the type she should be seen talking to, especially not now, with her reputation on the bubble. But she was too curious to hear what he was going to say—and how *she* was going to respond.

"I'm Reed," he said.

"Yeah, I know."

"Kaia and me, we—"

"Yeah, I know that, too." She didn't, not really. Kaia had never talked much about her life. But she'd dropped enough hints, and Harper had witnessed one kiss steamy enough to confirm that *something* was going on.

"I want to ask . . . I need to know . . ."

She felt a fist tighten around her heart. She'd been waiting for this, she realized. He would want to know all about it, what happened, every detail. *Did she suffer? Did she scream? Did she know?*

I don't remember! Harper wanted to shout. *I know what you know. Leave me alone.* But she stayed silent and kept her placid, patient smile fixed on her face. Maybe she wanted him to ask. At the very least, she could understand why he wanted to know: She did, too.

"Were you two, like, friends?"

"What?" It was so far from what she'd been expecting that it took her a moment to process.

"I don't know, I just thought—how are you, uh, doing?"

Harper let out a ragged breath, a precursor to a laugh or a sob—she wasn't sure which. What did he want, some kind of partner in crime for his adventures in grieving? As if the two of them would walk off hand in hand somewhere and cry on each other's shoulders? As if she could ever open up to someone like him?

If not him, then who?

"Uh, anyway, if you ever need, like, to talk—" He put a hand on her shoulder. A wave of emotion washed through her, and it wasn't the annoyance or revulsion she would have expected. It was comfort—and gratitude. *You too,* she wanted to say. But she couldn't force the words out.

"Ex*cuse* me?" Mini-She slammed three bottles of soda down on the table and advanced toward Reed, hands on hips. "What are *you* doing here?"

"Am I hallucinating, or are you, like, touching her?" Mini-Me chimed in, sliding a heaping lunch tray next to the drinks and joining her co-clone.

"You must be hallucinating," Mini-She pointed out, "because no way would someone like *him* be bothering someone like *us*."

"Don't you have, like, an engine to build?" Mini-Me asked. "Or some fires to set?"

"He's probably just begging for funds for his next pot buy," Mini-She suggested. She waved disdainfully. "Sorry, but charity hour's over for the day. Better luck next time."

Harper wanted to stop them, but if she did that, and took a stand, it would surely mean something—and she didn't have the energy to find out what.

"Yeah . . . ," Reed mumbled. "This was a mistake. Later."

"Try never!" Mini-Me called as he ambled away. Then she burst into giggles. "God, Harper, were you actually *talking* to that waste of space?"

"You're such an airhead," Mini-She taunted her friend. "She's Queen for a Day, remember? She was just waiting around for us to get rid of him for her."

"Which, by the way, you're welcome." Mini-Me did an exaggerated curtsy. "We're at your service, as always."

"Great job," Harper said weakly. She slumped into a chair at the nearest table. The giggle twins bounced down beside her.

"They didn't have Vitamin Water," Mini-She explained, pushing a handful of bottles across the table. "So I got you some Sprite, and Diet Coke, and some Poland Spring, and I can go back if you want something else. . . ."

"And the salad looked kind of dingy," Mini-Me added, setting a tray in front of Harper. It was piled high with a lump of brownish slime, surrounded by heaps of creamy beige sludge. "So I got you the . . . well, I'm not sure what it is, but there's plenty of protein. And then I got the mashed potatoes instead of the fries, you know, so there'd still be something healthy. . . ."

They gazed at her from across the table, identical expressions of nervous excitement trembling on their faces.

Harper felt sick at the thought of eating anything, especially the steaming heap sitting before her. She felt even sicker at the thought of sending the idiots away with a bitchy comment or two—much as she longed for some alone time, their words to Reed still hung in the air. They'd just been imitating her; she couldn't bring herself to repay the favor.

"This is great, guys," she said instead. "Everything's fine. Thanks." She grabbed the Sprite and took a fake sip. Ten minutes, she promised herself, and then she'd be up and out.

"You okay, Harper? You look kind of pale."

"Yeah, and no offense, but you're a little, like, sweaty. You sure you're okay?"

The more times she had to say it, the bigger the lie. But it's not like she had any other option.

"No worries," she assured them. "I'm fine."

"Beth, we still need a head for this article," the copy editor called out.

"And we're missing a photo for the Valentine's Day piece," the features editor called from the other side of the room.

Beth typed faster, trying to load in the changes to the front-page layout so she could deal with the hundred other things on her to-do list. It was times like this, rushing back and forth across the newsroom, slurping coffee, cutting and pasting, slapping on headlines, tweaking leads, and refereeing the occasional game of Nerf basketball, that she felt like a real editor in chief, the nerve center of a well-oiled fact-finding machine.

Then she remembered that, despite her best efforts, the paper rarely came out more than once a month—and when it did appear, its heartfelt missives on Homecoming Day hairdos and the debate team's latest victory ended up littering the floor of the cafeteria, crumpled and tossed aside before anyone had bothered to read them.

They weren't a complete failure, she reminded herself. They'd managed to get a special Kaia memorial supplement out a couple weeks ago, filling it—despite the short notice and lack of sources—with photos, poems, and the occasional testimonial from someone who professed to have known and loved "that dear, departed soul." Several of Beth's teachers had complimented her on the fine tribute. It wasn't the kind of compliment from which you could draw much joy—especially when you were still swimming in guilt.

Now things were back to normal, if you could call it normal when your front page featured an article about the sordid criminal past of the paper's former sponsor. Beth should have been pleased: It was just the kind of hard news she'd always imagined importing to the *Haven Gazette* when she finally took the reins. Along with all her other big plans, that dream had fallen by the wayside back in the fall, after her encounter with Mr. Powell.

Perhaps it was only fitting that, courtesy of Mr. Powell

and his misdeeds, the *Gazette* was finally reporting something that mattered.

Beth had long dreamed of covering a story like this, rich with tantalizing details and actual import. But not *this* story. She hadn't rushed an issue into print, hadn't assigned anyone to pester the cops or the administration for details. Instead, she'd just picked up the story that had run in the *Grace Herald* earlier that month. It would be reprinted verbatim. And it would have to do.

Student-Teacher Scandal Rocks Haven High
Police uncover secret identity as French teach skips town
By Milton Jeffries
Staff writer, *Grace Herald*

Massachusetts state police are pursuing Jack Powell, aka Julian Payne, for questioning in regard to two statutory rape cases allegedly involving the former Haven High School French teacher. Grace police are similarly eager to question him regarding his relationship with Kaia Sellers, a Haven High senior who was killed in a hit-and-run the same week Powell fled town. Police have ruled the incident an accident and concluded it was unconnected.

Powell joined the Haven High faculty in the fall, professing several years of teaching experience and proffering impeccable— and apparently forged—references. The first indication that anything was amiss came in late January, when an anonymous tip led paramedics to discover Powell unconscious in his apartment. Kaia Sellers's fingerprints were found at the scene, but she was killed the next day, before she could be questioned.

Powell's fingerprints, when run through a national database, revealed him to be Julian Payne, a British citizen who had disappeared from Stonehill, Massachusetts, six months earlier when allegations were made against him by two unnamed teenage girls.

Authorities at Stonehill Academy say that both girls are well-behaved, honor roll students who are to be commended for speaking out against their teacher. "We're all grateful that they had the courage [to turn Payne in] and prevent this from happening again," said Stonehill principal Patrick Darnton.

In Grace, area parents have expressed deep concern that a teacher with his background could have been employed by the high school; district officials say they had no sign Powell was not what he seemed.

Powell left the hospital, against medical advice, before Grace police were able to detain him. He has not been seen since.

She doesn't know why she came.

Hospitals have always seemed dirty to her, grimy, as if the grayish tinge to the walls and the floor were just germs made visible, layers of illness, fluids, and death that had built up over the years.

Still, she comes here often, forces herself to suffer through the candy striping, pediatric parties, holiday gift distributions. She knows where the bedpans are stored and which nurses ignore the call light. And she knows where all the exits are; from the moment she steps inside, she is always planning her escape.

She has come to see Harper, but she doesn't know why, and she doesn't have the nerve to go through with it. She steps off the elevator and starts down the hallway, but there is Adam, hovering outside the room next to the Graces, whom she recognizes because, in a small town, there is no one you don't know. She stops. She has nothing to say to any of these people. She has nothing to apologize for.

She has everything to apologize for.

Before she knows what she's doing, she turns around, is back at the elevators, pressing the button, waiting. It has been like this all week. Doing things without knowing why. Making decisions without even noticing. She wonders if she is in shock. Not over Kaia's death—none of that seems real yet; it all has the feel of a bad movie she wandered into that will surely end soon. No, if she is in shock, it is over what she has done, which is all too real and tangible, like the empty box on the edge of her nightstand that used to contain two yellow pills. She should throw it out, now that it's not just a box—now that it's evidence—but she can't bring herself to do so.

The elevator doors open and she steps on blindly, just as she does everything, which is why she doesn't see him until the doors close and it's too late.

"Now this is a pleasant surprise," he says, in the soft British accent she still hears in her nightmares. "And here I thought I'd have to leave without saying good-bye."

She ignores him. There is a vent in the ceiling of the elevator, and from a certain angle she can see through the slits and watch the walls of the shaft sliding by. There is a fan in the vent, its sharp blades spinning fast enough that they would slice off a finger if she were tall enough to reach.

"I'm fine, thanks for asking," he says. Unable to help herself, she glances toward him. There is a large white bandage on his forehead. His skin is pale. "Just a concussion, nothing to worry about."

"I wasn't," she says sharply.

He smiles at her, and then his face goes flaccid, his eyes flutter, and he stumbles backward, slamming into the console of buttons, catching himself just before he slumps to the floor. The elevator jerks to a stop. Beth says nothing, does nothing. He breathes deeply once, twice, as if willing the color back into his face and the strength back into his body. His head lolls to one side, and he grasps the railing on the wall for support. There is nothing Beth can do to help; she need not feel guilty for doing nothing.

She feels guilty for being glad about it.

More deep breaths, and soon, his face is no longer white, and the smile is back. And the elevator is not moving.

"I'm fine now," Powell says, touching his forehead gently. "Happens sometimes."

She doesn't say anything.

He steps away from the wall to look at the console. "I must have hit the emergency stop button. Not to worry, I'll have us moving again. Momentarily."

"You just need to flip the lever," Beth says, hating to acknowledge him but needing to escape. "It'll start up again."

Instead, he turns his back on the console and steps toward her. She jerks away, but of course, there is nowhere to go. Beth, who knows all the exits, knows that better than anyone.

"You're never sorry?" he asks, and he sounds almost plaintive.

"For what?"

"You misjudge me, you know." His voice is soft, and his eyes kind, as they were at the beginning, when the two of them worked long hours in the tiny newsroom, bent over layouts, their heads together. She'd called him Jack, cried on his shoulder, imagined what it might be like were she ten years older. She was no longer fooled. "We understood each other, or we could have. I could have taught you a lot. I could have been a friend. Things might have been . . ." He looks off to the side and sighs. "Different."

"Flip the lever," she says through gritted teeth. "Now."

"Scared?" He takes two rapid steps toward her and, before she can move, he's planted his arms on either side of her, pinning her against the wall. She is trembling. "You're a smart girl." His face is inches from hers, his breath sour. She knows she should do something. Spit. Scream. But she's frozen. "I could do anything." He leans closer, his eyes locked with hers. When their lips are about to touch, he stops. "But I won't."

His arms drop to his sides, and he steps backward again. "Disappointed?"

"Go to hell."

He shakes his head. "There's a part of you, Beth, that wants it. I knew it the moment we kissed—"

"When *you* kissed me," she snaps.

"When *we* kissed, I could tell. You want a lot of things you're not allowing yourself to want. You don't let yourself do anything about it, but that doesn't change the facts."

"You don't know anything about me," she whispers. Her throat is tight, as if she's having one of those dreams where she wants to scream but can't make a sound.

"I know girls," he says, nodding. A lock of brown hair flops over his eyes, and he brushes it away. The gesture reminds her of an old Hugh Grant movie. Adorable British charmer fumbles through life and gets the girl. She'd wanted a romantic-comedy life, maybe. But she hadn't wanted him, she insisted to herself, not really. She hadn't wanted this. "And I know you. You may be fooling everyone else with that good-girl act, Beth, but you can't fool me. I'm just sorry you felt you had to try."

He flips the lever, and the elevator jerks into motion.

As the doors open, he gives her a cheery salute. "Until we meet again . . . and something tells me we will."

She doesn't say good-bye.

Anyone with information about the whereabouts of Jack Powell or knowledge of his relationship with the late Kaia Sellers should contact the Grace Township Police Department, 555-4523.

"Beth, are we set with that article? We've got to lock the front page," the deputy editor reminded her.

She had an hour left before the paper went in for final proofing, then she had a history presentation to give, and afterward would rush off for yet another job interview, then home, where she could divide the rest of her night between studying for her math test, babysitting her little brothers, and working the phones to finalize logistics for Spirit Day and the senior auction.

She didn't have time to linger over Powell anymore. She clicks a button on the mouse and locks the article. "This one's set," she told her deputy. "Let's move on."

Miranda heard the chorus of blondes before she saw them, and their voices—high, flirtatious, infused with a permanent giggle and inevitably ending on a question mark—told her everything she needed to know. As she rounded the corner and approached the lockers, one look confirmed her suspicions. A harem of sophomores, outfitted in standard uniform: high boots, short skirt, midriff-baring shirt, and enough makeup to paint a house.

And there was Kane, towering above them, intense

brown eyes sparkling under his chiseled brow, and his smile . . . that smile was going to destroy her, Miranda often thought. It filled her daydreams—all her dreams, in fact— and rendered her powerless.

She was no better than any of these girls, except that she kept her simpering to herself. And look where it got her: They fluttered around the flame, and she lurked in the shadows, just passing through, nothing to see here but dull, drab Miranda.

She would just keep her head down, she told herself. Walk quickly and quietly down the hall and slip into study hall without anyone noticing her.

"Yo, Stevens! What's the hurry?"

She turned toward the syrupy smooth voice and at the sight of his familiar smirk was helpless not to favor him with one of her own.

"Looks like you've got your hands full at the moment," she told him, flicking a hand toward the girls.

"Beauties fit for a king, don't you think?" He gave them a magnanimous wave. "Ladies, you can take your leave for the moment—"

"But Kane, we're here to serve you," one of the blondes reminded him in a throaty voice.

"What if there's something you need?" another asked.

"And we can provide *anything* you need," the first reminded him.

"I'm sure Stevens here will take good care of me while you're gone."

The pom-pom posse looked her up and down. "Doubtful," one of them grouched. But they knew their role in this little drama: They followed orders and disappeared.

"That," Miranda began, shaking her head, "may be the most disgusting display I have ever seen."

Kane shrugged. "Give them a break—they're young, impressionable, and hey, it's hard not to go weak in the knees when you're in the presence of greatness."

"I'm not talking about them, your highness," Miranda snorted. "I'm talking about you. Could you be any more of a pig?"

He curled an arm around her shoulders and tugged her toward him. "You know you love it."

"How do you fit that huge ego into that tiny car of yours?" she teased.

"How do you fit that huge chip on your shoulder into that teeny tiny T-shirt?" he retorted.

Miranda blushed, pretending not to notice that *he'd* noticed her unusually snug shirt—though, of course, why else had she worn it?

"Don't give me that modest act," he chided her. "You know you look good." His hand glided down her back and Miranda caught her breath. "Sure you don't want to . . ."

God, did she want to. "We talked about this," she reminded him. She patted him on the shoulder and shook her head sympathetically. "It's so sad—no impulse control. Good thing I'm around to remind you of the rules."

"Rules are made to be—"

"Followed," she cut in. "Otherwise, why make them?"

And she was the one who'd made them, of course, much as she hated them. It was funny: She'd spent years hoping that Kane would notice that she'd grown past the tomboy phase and had actually sprouted a chest (sort of) and a healthy sex drive (at least when he was around). And now that he had finally noticed her—finally *kissed* her—she spent half her time fighting him off.

Okay, not so funny—more like tragic. But his brilliant friends-with-benefits plan had a few holes. One gaping hole, actually—the one that would appear after Miranda's heart shriveled up and disappeared, as it surely would after a few weeks, when Kane got bored of his no-strings-attached foreplay and moved on to his next conquest. She wanted more than that—she *deserved* more than that, she told herself, though she wasn't quite sure she believed it. She'd like to think she was pushing him away to preserve her dignity, but really, it was just self-protection.

So when he'd made a move, she'd made a rule:

No kissing.

Also: No fondling, flirting, or foreplay. No stroking, no tickling, no grabbing.

No fun, he'd pointed out. But then he'd shrugged and laughed. Your game, your rules, he'd said.

Since then, they'd gone back to their default mode of snarky banter—with a twist. Now half the time the banter was tinged with sexual innuendo, and occasionally, when bored, Kane seemed to enjoy testing their new boundaries. "Does this count as a kiss?" he'd ask, playfully whispering in her ear with his lips against her skin. "Is this stroking, or just heavy petting?" he'd tease, smoothing down her long, reddish hair.

Sometimes, she suspected that knowing she was off limits actually made him want her more; sometimes she suspected that had been her plan all along.

In the meantime, she pretended it was all a game, one

whose outcome didn't faze her one way or the other. She pretended that, like him, she was putting aside lust for the good of their growing friendship; hoping he'd never suspect the true four-letter L word that lay behind it all. It was torture, but the sting was sweet and sharp, like when you bit your tongue and then couldn't stop worrying the tender spot against your teeth, half enjoying the taste of pain.

"When are you going to loosen up, Stevens?" he asked, heaving a sigh that she knew was all for show.

"As soon as you grow up, Geary."

"Never!" He leaped back with a look of horror, then whipped out a pen and posed, brandishing it as if it were a sword. "Just call me Peter Pan."

Miranda grinned despite herself. "My very own lost boy. Aren't I lucky?"

"And you, lovely lady, can be my Wendy . . . or perhaps you'd prefer Tinkerbell?"

"Tinkerbell? Give me a break." Miranda winked; then, in a single, lightning-quick gesture, snatched the pen out of his hand while circling behind him, wrapped an arm around his waist, and pressed the edge of the pen against his neck as if it were a blade. "More like Captain Hook."

"Mr. Morgan," the secretary said, eyeing him suspiciously, "she'll see you now. Go right in."

Adam sighed and stuffed his iPod back into his backpack. Secretaries used to love him—but then, that was back when he only got called down to the administrative wing to pick up his latest trophy or talk to some local reporter about breaking an all-school record. He was even trotted out at the occasional school board meeting, an example for the community of Haven High's "exceptional athletic organization." But ever since starting an on-court brawl and getting suspended for a week, Adam had noticed a definite chill in his relationship with the administration, including the secretaries.

That's all behind me now, Adam reminded himself. He'd been angry—*too* angry—for a long time. After everything had happened, he'd resolved to get some control over himself. Forgive, forget, chill out. Get his act together. And it was working . . . so far.

He slung his backpack over one shoulder and stood up, trudging slowly toward the guidance counselor's door. Of all the doors in all the offices in all Haven High, this was his least favorite. Ms. Campbell didn't care if he'd broken the butterfly relay record or led the basketball team to its first regional championship in a decade. All she ever wanted to talk about was his classes, his work, his SATs— and all she ever wanted to know was how he could accept being so subpar. She wouldn't accept it, she always promised him. What she didn't get was that *he* didn't accept it, either. But he didn't know what else he was supposed to do.

"Come in, Adam. Sit down." She waved him in, offering him a decrepit hard candy from the overflowing china dish at the edge of her desk. He waved it away. An elderly, overweight woman whose gray hair and wire-rimmed glasses gave her an unfortunate resemblance to Ben Franklin, Ms. Campbell served as a part-time health teacher, part-time English teacher, part-time PTA liaison, and full-time busybody. She'd been the Haven High guidance counselor for thirty years—which made a fair number of students question her guidance-giving credentials. Not to mention her sanity. Three decades in Haven's hallowed halls wouldn't represent a bright future; it sounded more like a prison sentence.

Ms. Campbell pushed a mound of clutter across her desk—Adam caught a snow globe moments before it crashed to the ground—making room for his permanent file. She flipped it open and peered at him over the rims of her glasses.

"How are things going, Adam?" she asked, frowning. "Anything happening in your life? Any concerns you'd like to express?"

Was anything happening? Aside from his two best friends teaming up to ruin his life? Aside from breaking up with one girl, falling in love with another, then breaking up again, all in the space of a month? Aside from one of those girls almost dying in a car crash and then refusing to speak to him?

And, oh yeah, aside from the fact that the girl to whom he'd lost his virginity had ended up *dead*, and he was still having dreams about the night he'd spent with her—dreams that turned into nightmares as her flesh burned away in his arms?

Aside from that?

"Nothing much." Adam shrugged. "Just, you know, the usual."

"Well, *I* have some concerns," she said. "Maybe we can talk about that." She began flipping through the file. "Your grades have never been . . . let's just say you've never worked up to your full potential."

Guidance counselors loved that kind of talk. Potential.

Aspirations. Opportunity. None of it meant anything to Adam. It was all just a bunch of abstract bullshit designed to make you play along with their game and do whatever they said. He didn't need the stress; he was happy just hanging with his friends and playing ball, and the rest would take care of itself.

"But this year, your teachers have alerted me to a distinct dip in your grades," Ms. Campbell said. She looked up from the file and fixed him with a sharp gaze. "Are you aware that you're failing most of your classes?"

"Uh . . . no." He began to tense up, realizing this wasn't going to be some generic meeting he could just ignore. He'd never had the best grades—but he'd never failed before, either. Of course, in the past, he'd had Beth by his side, forcing him to get the work done, and to do it right. Now he was on his own.

"What are your plans for the future, Adam?"

"The future?" Another one of those words guidance counselors liked to toss around, as if the future was really something you could plan for. If he'd learned anything this year, he'd learned that was a joke.

"Next year. We've only got a few months until graduation. Have you thought at all about what you're going to do?"

Adam shifted uncomfortably in his seat. He preferred not to think about graduation, and the gray space that lay beyond it. He'd ignored the whole college applications thing. There was always community college, down the road in Ludlow, or the state school in Borrega. More school just seemed like a waste of time. He liked being outside. He liked playing ball. He liked working with his hands.

College wasn't going to help much with any of that.

"There's plenty of time," he muttered.

"Too many people your age don't consider the future," she lectured. "You're just aimless wanderers, stuck in the moment, as if nothing's ever going to change, as if you'll never have any responsibilities. These days it's all about instant gratification, what can I have *right now*. And what with all the drugs, alcohol, sex . . ."

After an uncomfortably long pause, Adam wondered whether she was waiting for him to respond.

"Uh . . . Ms. Campbell?" She nodded expectantly. "I guess, I'm, uh, not sure where you're going with this?"

She snapped the file shut and stood up. "Where I'm going is this," she said in an unusually firm voice. "Your grades are atrocious, and you're in danger of failing the year. I'm assigning you a tutor, and with some hard work, I hope you'll be able to dig yourself out of this hole."

"A tutor?" He was aware of the whiny note that had crept into his voice, but couldn't help himself. How lame could you get? "Do I have to?"

"You don't *have* to do anything, Adam."

He smiled in relief.

"But without a tutor, your grades won't improve. And if your grades don't improve, *soon*, you can stop worrying about your future. Because you're not going to graduate."

Miranda was about to open the stall door when she heard their voices. Mini-She's was a bit higher than Mini-Me's, but otherwise, they were interchangeable. Just like the rest of them.

"She's such a bitch."

"Totally."

"Do you think she even knows what people are saying about her?"

A sigh. "It's tragic."

"Totally."

"I mean, she was the shit."

"Definitely."

"But all that crazy stuff last month?"

"Total meltdown."

"And poor Kaia . . ."

"She probably went crazy and ran them both off the road."

A moment of silence.

"That was all really sad."

"Yeah."

"That was kind of a hot skirt she was wearing today, though. Think it would look good on me?"

"Totally. And I was thinking I might pick up one of those tank tops—"

"You bitch! I was all over that."

"No prob, I'll go green, you stick with the blue."

Giggles.

"I feel kind of bad for her, you know?"

"Oh, yeah, me too, of course."

"That's why I'm totally going to stick by her."

"Oh, yeah, me too, of course."

"It's like a community service project or something."

"God, that's sad."

"Tragic."

"Good thing she's got friends like us."

"Totally."

The door banged shut, and then there was silence.

Miranda held her breath and opened the door of the stall. The girls' room was empty. She squirted some soap into her hands, ran them under the hot water, and waited.

She'd just reached for a paper towel when a second stall door opened, and Harper finally emerged.

Harper washed her hands in silence. Miranda could tell she was nibbling on the inside of her left cheek, a nervous habit. She bent down, and then flipped her head up again, her hair flying back down to her shoulders. She ran a hand through, fluffing up the sides and smoothing it down at the roots. "I'm thinking of getting it cut," Harper said finally. "Nothing too dramatic, though."

"Sounds good," Miranda said, waiting for some kind of explosion.

Harper pulled out a tube of cherry-colored lipstick.

"Nice color," Miranda told her. "New?"

"Yeah. Want to try?"

"I don't know." She looked in the mirror, giving her limp hair a disdainful flip. Cherry and orange didn't seem like a match made in heaven. "Think it would look good on me?"

Harper tossed over the tube, then raised her eyebrows and gave Miranda a weak half smile. "Totally."

chapter

4

It wasn't easy to surprise Kane Geary. When you assume that everyone in the world is out for themselves, not much happens that you don't see coming.

But this was most definitely unexpected.

Beth sat at a table just in front of the school doors, handing out Haven High pennants and wrist bands to any seniors who'd forgotten to dress in Haven's school colors—rust and mud—for Spirit Day; the most festively adorned, psychotically spirited senior would win some kind of fabulous grand prize.

Kane wore a navy button-down shirt and Michael Kors jeans.

He didn't do spirit.

Harper was a few feet ahead of him, walking quickly with her head down, taking a few final puffs on her cigarette before entering the school. Kane, who noticed everything, caught Beth looking away as she approached—no surprise there. Harper, on the other hand, barely noticed the table of paraphernalia or the blond beauty staffing it. She just took one last drag and carelessly flicked the cigarette away—too carelessly, it turned out, as it tumbled through the air, right into Ms. Barbini's back.

Never a good idea to pelt the teachers with cigarettes—tempting as it often was—but Ms. Barbini, the no-nonsense, no-deodorant geometry teacher, was a particularly poor choice. She whirled around, bent down, and picked up the incriminating butt between her thumb and index finger, then glared at Harper, who had frozen in place.

"Who threw this?" she asked, in a tone that suggested she need not wait for an answer.

Kane was close enough to see Harper roll her eyes, open her mouth . . . and snap it shut again as Beth leaped to her feet.

"I did, Ms. Barbini," she announced.

Surprise.

Kane and Ms. Barbini goggled at her; Harper's face remained expressionless, as if she were watching a rather boring show on TV and was just waiting for a commercial.

"You?" the teacher said incredulously.

"Me."

"Can I go now?" Harper asked. "Wouldn't want to be late for homeroom." She shot a hostile glare at Beth—a silent message that looked less like *thank you* and more like *your choice, your funeral*—and, without waiting for an answer, limped up the stairs and disappeared inside the school.

"I'm very disappointed in you, Ms. Manning. Smoking on school grounds?" The teacher whipped out a small pink pad and began to scribble. "That's two days' detention." She thrust the detention slip at Beth and, after giving her a disdainful scowl, followed in Harper's footsteps up the stairs and through the heavy wooden doors.

It had been a late night, and Kane had almost cut homeroom to sleep in—good thing he'd made the "responsible" choice, as nothing cured a hangover like a good mystery. And there was nothing more mysterious than Beth taking the fall for her mortal enemy.

"Now *that* was interesting," he said, sauntering up to Beth's table. He swept aside a swath of orange and brown crap and hopped on, half standing, half sitting, and all in Beth's face.

"Good morning," she chirped, her face a gruesome imitation of a smile. "Would you like a pennant?"

"I'd like to know if you're lobbying for sainthood."

The smile collapsed into a frown—this one looked real. "Get off of there." A pause. "Please."

"She's not going to thank you," Kane pointed out. "But you know that. And you've got no reason to want to help her, unless maybe you just feel sorry for her . . . but even the kind and generous Beth Manning wouldn't go *that* far." He leaned toward her, squinting as if to peer more deeply into her eyes and uncover the real motive.

"Can you just leave me alone?" Beth snapped. Her face was turning pale, and she looked nervously down at the stack of papers she was shuffling and reshuffling as she spoke.

"If I didn't know better, I'd think you owed her in some way," Kane mused. "But what could *you* possibly owe *Harper?*"

At first, he'd just been enjoying himself watching her squirm—but Kane was beginning to suspect that his instincts were right, and something really was going on here. And it turned out that, accompanying his natural curiosity was an uncharacteristically sincere urge to protect Harper from whatever it might be. The second surprise of the morning.

"Just drop it," she pleaded in a choked voice. "Just go away."

"Where's all this hostility coming from?" He gave her a wounded look. "I thought we were supposed to be *friends* now—isn't that what you said?"

"Forget what I—"

"Is this jerk bothering you?"

Ah, the knight in shining armor, Kane thought, without turning around. Just in time.

"Chill out, buddy," he told Adam. "Your ex and I are just having a little chat." Kane stopped, and then, laughing as if the thought had just occurred to him, continued, "I guess she's *my* ex too. Share and share alike."

"Get out of here, Kane." Adam grabbed him roughly by the shoulder and pulled him off the table. Kane wrestled his arm away, but that was it. He didn't leave; he also didn't fight back. Adam was the one with the problem, Adam was the one with the grudge—Adam was the one who, despite an apology and plenty of time, refused to get over it. He liked to act the wounded party, but he was the one who'd called an official end to their friendship. Over a *girl*. Adam was the one who just couldn't deal.

"You okay, Beth?" he asked now, pulling that Mr. Sensitive act the girls couldn't get enough of. (Except for Beth, Kane noted, with more than a flicker of pride— thanks in part to him, she'd had plenty.)

"I don't need you to protect me," she snapped, rising from the table.

"Can't you both see that I'm busy?" she cried suddenly. "I'm taking care of a million things, and the two of you . . ." She slammed down the cover of her thick binder and grabbed it off the table, hugging it to her chest.

"Beth—" Adam smiled and held up his hands in supplication.

"No. Not now. Just leave me alone. *Both* of you." No one moved. "No? Fine, then I'll do it for you."

She spun away, her blond hair whipping against Kane's face, and walked off.

Kane and Adam stared at each other, Adam looking like he'd just taken a swig of sour milk.

"So," he said finally, rubbing a hand against his close-cropped blond hair.

"Yeah," Kane agreed.

"What did you—?"

"Hey, nothing," Kane protested quickly, shaking his head. "She's just wound too tight."

"Ya think?" Adam laughed, sounding not particularly happy, but not particularly angry, either, which was a change. "I'm starting to think all girls are crazy. She 'forgive' you, too?"

Kane nodded, and the two exchanged a wry smile, their first in weeks. "Wonder what she acts like when she holds a grudge."

Adam was waiting for his tutor in the "computer lab" (really a closet-size space with a couple of stone-age PCs) when Miranda wandered in.

Great. Just great.

He'd hoped to keep the whole humiliating tutor thing

under wraps, but if Miranda got wind of it, surely she'd run straight to Harper—who, in her current mood, might spread it all over school.

More good luck for me, he thought sourly.

"Hey, Adam." Miranda didn't look particularly surprised to see him, just uncomfortable. "What's up?"

"Just waiting for someone," he said brusquely, hoping she'd take the hint and leave.

And then the other shoe dropped—on his head.

"Uh, yeah . . . I know." She gave him a tight smile, and the truth sunk in.

"*You're* my tutor?"

"Guilty." Miranda rubbed the back of her neck and hovered in the doorway. "Look, if this is too weird for you or anything, I'm sure you could get them to assign you someone else—"

"No, no," he said without thinking, not wanting to be rude. But, on second thought . . . he'd known Miranda for years, and though they'd never been close, they'd always had one big thing in common: Harper.

Maybe this wasn't such bad luck after all.

"I'm glad it's you," he told her, "and not some jerk who'd go bragging to the honor society about what an idiot I am."

Miranda set her stuff down and pulled up a chair. "You're not an idiot," she said firmly.

Adam spit out a laugh. "I can see Campbell didn't give you the full story. Trust me," he boasted, clasping his hands together over his head like a champion, "you're looking at the official winner of the Haven High dumbass award."

"I'm sure it's not that bad," Miranda said, grinning.

Adam was suddenly certain that she didn't know he was on the verge of not graduating; he wasn't about to fill her in.

"So, where should we start?" she asked.

He shrugged. "I guess I've got a math test this week," he mumbled. Most of his friends were in calc or pre-calc this year, but he was stuck taking basic algebra. It was really for juniors—and it was still way over his head.

"Cool, I love math." As the words slipped out, Miranda looked up, horrified. "You tell anyone I just said that and I'll have to kill you."

"How about a deal?" he suggested. "You keep this whole tutoring thing to yourself and I won't tell anyone that you're secretly a total geek."

They grinned, and shook on it.

That was the end of the fun—Miranda dove right into the work, struggling to explain to Adam how to apply the quadratic formula and what it meant when an equation had an imaginary solution. But he couldn't focus, and not just because it all sounded like a foreign language.

"How is she?" he asked suddenly, looking up from the books.

Miranda didn't even pretend to be confused. "She's okay. . . ." She sighed. "That's what she says, at least. I don't ask anymore. It's just . . . it's better that way, you know?"

"Yeah." He didn't know, of course. But he knew Harper, so he could imagine.

"Have you talked to her? I mean, have you two been . . . ?"

"You don't know?" Adam wrinkled his forehead. "I thought girls talked all that stuff to death."

"Well, lately . . ."

"Yeah," he said again. "Lately." He wouldn't make her say it. "She won't talk to me," he admitted. "I don't know why."

But that was a lie, wasn't it? He knew exactly why—he couldn't accept it.

She looks much better this time. Her skin is pink, her breathing strong and steady, the machines gone. And her eyes are open.

For two days, she refused to see anyone. And then, today, he was summoned.

She waves weakly when he comes into the room. She doesn't smile.

"You look good, kid," he says. Comparatively, it is true.

"They say I'm going home tomorrow."

"Great!" His smile feels fake. Hers is nonexistent.

He comes over to the bed and leans over, giving her a kiss on the forehead. "I'm really glad you're okay, Harper," he says softly. "I'm—" He doesn't know how to talk about it, what it felt like to lie awake in bed worrying about her, not knowing, waiting for something to happen, desperately hoping it wouldn't, but even more desperate for the weird, endless, torturous limbo of waiting to just end. One way or another. He doesn't want to ask if she heard all the things he told her when her eyes were closed, because he's afraid that she did—and afraid that she didn't. "We were all really worried," he says finally, hiding in the "we."

"I didn't think you'd come," she says dully. "I thought you hated me."

"Of course I don't hate you," he says, his voice too jolly. She winces. He knows he's trying too hard; he just doesn't know what he's trying to do. He pulls a familiar chair up to the bed. He doesn't take her hand. "Look, things got all screwed up at the end

there, and I . . . we both said a lot of things that . . . you know, we probably shouldn't have."

"Mostly you said a lot of things," she reminds him. "I just said I'm sorry."

She'd said it over and over again; he hadn't wanted to listen.

"I know. I know you are," he tells her. "I get that now. And I forgive you."

"Really?" Her eyes widen. She tries to sit up in bed, and her face twists in pain. He touches her shoulder, gently, helping her to lie back. She reaches out, touches his face. "Everything I did, I just did it because—"

"I know."

The tension disappears from her face. "Then it's okay," she murmurs, almost to herself. "Then at least something is . . ."

He leans in closer, struggling to hear—and she kisses him.

He jerks away.

He does it without even thinking.

He hasn't thought any of it through, he realizes now. And now it's too late.

"What?" There is a new pain on her face. "What is it?"

"Gracie, when I said—I didn't mean—"

"You said you forgave me, Ad," she says softly, as if maybe he forgot, and this is all a simple misunderstanding. "So that's it. We can start again. No more lies, no more—"

"No." He doesn't know he's going to say it before the word pops out, but he means it. "I want us to be friends again, Harper, I really do. But anything else . . . I think we work better, just as friends. When we tried to have more"—When you had to have more, he doesn't say—"things got messy."

"But it was all a mistake!" she protests, her voice scratchy and weak. "I explained that. I apologized, a million times. And you *just want to go back? Like none of it ever happened? Like you never told me that you—"*

"None of it was real." He tries not to look away. He wants so much to make her smile; but he can't tell her what she wants to hear. "When we were together, it was all a lie." The words are harsh, but his voice is gentle. He doesn't want to hurt her. "Everything you said was based on lies—and everything I said, that was just because I believed them."

She sags back against the pillows, her face returning to the dull, expressionless mask she'd worn when he came in.

Stop, he tells himself, horrified. Look what he's said, what he's done. He has to fix it—fix her.

"Gracie, you're my best friend," he says, and now he does take her hand. He can feel her pulling away, but he squeezes tighter, and she doesn't have the strength. "I miss that. I miss you. We tried the whole dating thing, and it didn't work out. It doesn't matter why, or whose fault it is. It just didn't. But that doesn't mean—"

"Get out," she says flatly.

"What?"

"I don't need this."

"I don't understand," he says, trying not to.

"You don't forgive me," she says bitterly. "You still think I'm not good enough for you, that I'm this manipulative slut who can't be trusted. That's what you told me, isn't it? That I'm this terrible person, all rotted on the inside?"

"But I was wrong," he protests. "I didn't mean it."

"Right." Her voice swells, and he realizes that even now, hurt, powerless, confined to a bed, she has power. She is still, after all, Harper Grace. "You meant it. Then. So what's changed now? You see me lying here and you feel sorry for me? You figure poor

little Harper needs a nice pick-me-up in her bed of pain? And what? I'm supposed to be grateful for your pity?" Her voice is shaking, but her eyes are dry. And he knows that she will never let him see her pain.

"It's not pity," he argues.

"Yeah, but it's not—" She stops herself. There is a long silence. "You don't have to worry about me," she says finally. "I'm fine. You did your little good deed by coming here, so you can forget your guilty conscience."

It would be so easy to fix this, he thinks. All he has to do is take her back, tell her he loves her and he understands everything she did to him. Tell her he's ready to start over again, that the past doesn't matter.

But it does matter. A car crash can't erase anything that happened, or the choices that she made; it doesn't change the kind of person she is, it doesn't make it any easier to trust her again.

"You should get some rest," he says. "We can talk about this tomorrow. I'll come back and—"

"Don't."

"I want to."

"I don't care." She turns her head away from him and closes her eyes. They're done.

"She's feeling a lot better," Miranda said, shrugging. "I'm sure pretty soon everything else will be back to normal. And the two of you . . ."

"I don't know," he said dubiously, although he had the same hope. It's why he kept trying, in hopes that, if nothing else, she'd eventually get tired of pushing him away.

"I could tell her you were asking," Miranda offered.

"No, don't bother." He looked down at his notebook, where a mess of numbers and letters sprinkled the page in

69

an incomprehensible pattern. "Maybe we should just get back to work."

After all, nothing in his life made much sense anymore; at least when it came to algebra, there was an answer key in the back of the book.

Beth pressed her foot down on the gas pedal, nudging the car just over the speed limit, and tried not to think about the two meetings she was blowing off or the stack of homework she'd face when she got home again. Today had gone from bad—an encounter with Kane that had rattled her even more than her first ever detention slip— to worse as she'd bombed a pop quiz, forgotten her gym uniform, and almost lost the Spirit Day prizes. She'd found them at the last minute, but had been forced to miss the culminating Spirit Rally in favor of her first detention, where she'd cowered in the back row under the glare of a tall, gaunt boy with pale skin and greasy hair who kept whispering something about how hot she'd look in leather.

It would be nice to say it had all been worth it, that she'd managed to erase some part of her imagined debt to Harper, and she was able to start feeling good about herself again, or at the very least that she could put the day behind her, sleep long and hard, and hope the next day would be better.

But she just felt unsteady. Maybe it was the detention, maybe it was the four cups of coffee she'd downed since morning, maybe it was Kane—her *supplier*, she reminded herself. She tried to shut it out, but the image popped into her mind yet again: the empty box on her nightstand. Kane was the only one who knew about it—the only one who could ever suspect what she'd done.

And if he hadn't given her the pills, she reminded herself, none of this would have happened. She hated him—almost as much as she hated herself.

Little wonder that she couldn't face her meeting, haggling with a bunch of overly enthusiastic volunteers about how to stage the next day's auction, where to hang the banners, which last-minute details to delegate and which to ditch. It was too depressing, especially since she used to be one of them, trying hard, worrying, taking all that nervous energy left over from waiting for college decisions and funneling it into something productive and mildly entertaining. Now she was just acting the part. And it was getting old.

She couldn't face going home; the house was always either too full of people, noise, and clutter to think straight, or it was empty and too quiet.

So she'd driven away, following the familiar curves until she reached the spot that guaranteed her a quiet place to think. She felt guilty there, as if she were trespassing, especially in those moments when she was overcome by self-pity—it felt wrong, feeling sorry for herself, there of all places. But she couldn't help it. And as time passed, it became the only place that could help.

The road curved, and the thin white cross appeared. Beth pulled her car onto the shoulder and parked. She hesitated for a moment, staring through the windshield at the small wooden cross stuck into the brush-covered ground, the withering bunches of flowers gathered around it. It looked almost lonely, dwarfed by the vast emptiness of the surrounding desert. From this distance she couldn't see the name scratched into the wood, but she imagined she could. She had traced her fingers over the letters often enough.

Beth didn't know who had erected the small memorial—Kaia's father, from the few glimpses she'd gotten before he left town, didn't seem the type. And there were few other candidates. She got out of the car and walked slowly over to the cross, then sat on the ground in front of it, not caring if she got dirt all over her jeans. She'd brought along her ancient duct-taped-together Discman, and now she switched it on, sliding the headphones over her head and tuning out the world.

The first time she'd come, she had wandered through the brush, looking for signs that something had happened here. And she'd found them—small spots of scorched earth, scratches and gouges in the ground, a smear of rubber on the road, a jagged chunk of metal, twisted and torn beyond recognition. But all of that was gone now; or, at least, Beth no longer had any urge to look. Now she just sat and stared, sometimes at the roughly engraved letters—just KAIA, no dates, no messages, no last name—sometimes at the empty road and still scenery, disturbed only by the occasional eighteen-wheeler barreling through, sometimes at the sky. She chose her music at random, though most of the CDs in her collection were weepy women, singer-songwriters warbling about lost love, so there was rarely much surprise. Today, however, she'd popped in an old Green Day album—something Adam had given her in hopes of giving her some kind of music makeover. She'd never really listened to it. But it was loud and angry, and today, somehow, it worked.

It's not my fault, she told herself, trying to dislodge the mountain of guilt. There was no cause and effect. No connection. She'd drugged Harper; Kaia had crashed a car. It was a coincidence, nothing more. A bad driver, speeding down the road, slamming into the BMW, disappearing. It was an accident—just bad luck. *Not my fault.* Harper was fine. Harper was healthy. Whatever Beth had done, there'd been no permanent consequences.

What happened to Kaia was permanent, but—*not my fault.*

She didn't know how long she'd been sitting there when she felt the hand on her shoulder. She tipped her head back and looked up into the deepest brown eyes she'd ever seen. She took in his warm, crooked smile, the tendrils of dark, curly hair that flopped over his eyes, the smudge of grease just above his chin . . . and then it all came together into a familiar face, and she jerked away.

"Hey," he said, his voice warm and gravelly, as if he'd just rolled out of bed. "Sorry." He sat down next to her. "Didn't mean to scare you."

"You didn't," Beth said, pulling off her headphones. She couldn't look at him.

Reed flicked his eyes toward the cross. "I didn't know anyone else came here," he said. "Didn't think anyone cared." He spoke slowly, pausing between each word as if part of him preferred the silence. "I didn't know you two were friends."

Beth couldn't bring herself to say that they weren't, that Kaia had zoomed to the top of Beth's enemies list by sleeping with her boyfriend; she couldn't admit the hours she'd spent wishing Kaia Sellers out of existence. But she also didn't want to lie.

"I'm Reed," he said, breaking the awkward silence. "Maybe you don't remember, but we met a while ago, before . . ." He reached for her hand and shook it, an oddly formal gesture considering they were sitting across from each other in the dirt on the side of a highway. His hand was warm, his grip tight; she didn't want to let go.

"I remember." She'd been upset, and he'd cheered her up, somehow—she couldn't remember now. Couldn't even remember what she'd been so upset about. It felt like a different lifetime. "I should go," she said suddenly, realizing he probably wanted to be alone—she didn't belong. "Do you want me to—?"

"I should take off," he said at the same time. They both stopped talking and laughed, then, shooting a guilty glance at the thin, white cross, fell into silence again.

"Really, I should go," she insisted.

"No, stay." He sighed and rubbed a worn spot on the knee of his jeans where the denim was about to tear apart. "Please."

Beth nodded, feeling her chest tighten. *It's not my fault. I didn't do this.*

The sun was already setting, but it was a cloudless day, so there was no brilliant sunset, only a steadily deepening haze as the sun dipped beneath the horizon. Reed dug around in his pocket and pulled out a flat, grayish stone, its edges rounded and its top streaked with red. He stood up, placed it in front of the cross, where it was lost amid the bouquets of dying flowers. Then he sat down again and gave Beth a half smile. "I saw it, somewhere, that people do that. And I just thought it was, you know, a good thing to do."

Beth opened her mouth to say, "That's nice." Instead, she let out a gasping sob and burst into tears.

"Hey," Reed said, sounding alarmed. "Hey, don't—"

Beth had squeezed her eyes shut, willing the tears to stop, so she didn't see him leaning toward her. She just felt his strong arms pull her in, pressing her head against his chest.

"It's okay," he murmured, stroking her hair. "It's okay."

He smelled sweet and smoky and, as her gasps quieted, she could hear his heart beat.

"I miss her too," he whispered.

Oh, God.

"I'm sorry," she blurted, her voice muffled by his shirt. She pushed him away and stood up. "I have to go, I'm sorry." By the time he stood up, she'd already started running toward her car, tears blinding her vision.

She didn't know if he was trying to follow her and, as she started the car and tore out onto the road, she forced herself not to care. She never should have allowed him to comfort her like that, and she couldn't let it happen again.

She didn't deserve it.

Harper jerked awake, her breath ragged, sweat pouring down her face. She turned over to check the clock: 2:46 a.m. Four hours to go before the rest of the house woke up, and she would hear some noises other than her pounding heart.

She felt like she was still trapped in the nightmare; the dark shadows of her room seemed alive with possibility, as if the childhood monsters she'd once feared had returned to haunt her. But that was just the dream talking, she reminded herself. And nightmares weren't real.

Except.

Except that her nightmares were memories that fled as soon as she opened her eyes. All she had were glimpses: the scream of tearing metal, the stench of smoke, the heavy weight on her chest that made it hurt to breathe. Her pillow was damp, maybe with sweat—she rubbed her eyes—maybe with tears.

She should be used to it by now, and she ran through her regular routine: Lying still, on her back, eyes fixed on the ceiling, counting her breaths. It was supposed to relax her and lull her back to sleep, but this time, it relaxed some protective barrier in her mind, and the images of her nightmare came flooding back.

Harper sat up. "No." It was halfway between a plea and a moan. "Please."

But the truth slammed into her. She squeezed her eyes shut and fell forward, clapping a hand over her mouth, fighting against her sudden nausea.

Deep breaths, she told herself, trying to stop shaking.

It was only a dream.

Except it wasn't a dream and she *couldn't* breathe. She felt like someone had shoved a gasoline-soaked rag into her mouth and she was choking on rough cotton and toxic fumes.

If it was true, she thought, *I'd light the match.*

She'd waited so long to remember, but now she fought against it; maybe she could hide in the dark, she told herself, slip back into sleep, and wake up the next morning, everything safely forgotten.

But she stood up and fumbled her way toward the desk, refusing to turn on a light—that would make it too real. Blinking back tears, she found the business card and brought it back to her bed, reading the numbers by the dim light of her clock radio. Her fingers hesitated over the buttons on her cell. She had to do it now, she told herself; in the morning, in the light, she'd be too afraid.

The phone rang and rang, and then, just before she was about to hang up, the voice mail kicked in.

"This is Detective Sharon Wells. Leave your name and phone number after the beep. If this is an emergency, please call 911."

"This is Harper Grace," she said quickly, thinking, *This is* an emergency. She tried not to let her voice shake. "You told me to call you if I remembered anything. About, you know, the accident. And. I did."

Harper snapped the phone shut and dove back into bed, burrowing under the covers. She squeezed her eyes closed but couldn't force the images out of her brain.

Kaia laughing.

The truck barreling toward them.

Music pumping.

Breaks squealing.

And Harper's hands wrapped around the wheel.

chapter

5

"I need to talk to you. *Now*," Harper hissed.

Pretending not to notice the urgency in her voice, Kane tossed some books into his locker and eased the door shut. "At your service," he told her, leaning against the cool metal and waiting for her to unload.

"Not here." She looked up and down the hallway—students were trickling into the classrooms and there wasn't a teacher in sight. "Come on."

Not like he had much choice in the matter. She grabbed his sleeve and dragged him down the hall, slipping through a side door and depositing him on a small landing behind the history wing. It was an emergency exit whose alarm had been conveniently disabled, and since the stairwell down led to a narrow plot of cement bordered by a concrete retention wall, it was unlikely they'd be noticed.

"So what's the emergency?" He perched on the railing and, letting himself tip backward, idly wondered how far he'd be able to lean before gravity pulled him all the way down.

"You want to tell me again what you saw?" Harper asked, pacing back and forth on the narrow landing. Her hair, more unruly than usual, flowed out behind her, and Kane suddenly noticed that she wasn't wearing any makeup. His grin faded; Harper didn't go for the natural look. Ever.

"Saw when?" he asked. "You're going to have to give me a little more to go on here."

"The accident." She spit out. "In the parking lot, the day—you know when. What you told the cops. Tell *me*."

Kane stretched his mouth wide open, cracking his jaw, then sighed. "I saw Kaia drive up to the school," he began in a mechanical voice. The recitation of events had by now become so familiar, he'd memorized the spiel. "I saw you run out of the school. You talked for a while. Then you got into the car and Kaia drove away."

"Bullshit!" Harper snapped. "Want to try again?"

"That's the only story I've got," Kane protested. "So unless you want me to make something up . . ."

"You? Lie?" She made a noise that could have been a laugh. "Wouldn't want to make you do that."

She stopped pacing suddenly, and slumped against the brick wall of the school, facing Kane. Her chest shuddered as she gasped for air; how fast did you have to be breathing, Kane wondered, before you were officially hyperventilating?

"Chill out, Grace. What's with you?"

"What did you *see*, Kane? Not what you told the police. What *happened*?"

She knew something, he could hear it in her tone. Kane swung off the railing and approached her. "What. Are. You. Talking. About," he said, slowly and clearly, overenunciating, hoping that if he couldn't tease away her mood, he could piss her off enough that she'd snap out of it.

"When I woke up in the hospital, I didn't remember anything that happened," Harper said.

"I know." He said it casually, as if it were no big deal that she was talking about this, despite the fact that until now, it had been clearly marked as off-limits, surrounded by conversational barbed wire.

"They just told me what—" She closed her eyes for a moment and, drawing in a deep breath, set her mouth in a firm line as if readying herself for a blow. "They told me she died. She was driving, there was some other car, there was a crash, and she . . . died."

"It sucks." Kane shifted his weight back and forth, waiting for the point.

"Why'd you do it?" she asked softly.

"What?"

"That's what I don't get. What's in it for you?"

"What the hell are you talking about, Harper?"

"I remembered."

Now Kane closed his eyes, then opened them again, searching her face for . . . uncertainty? Vulnerability? Gratitude? He didn't know, and whatever he was looking for, it wasn't there. Her face was angry, and that was it.

"Last night," she said, "I had a nightmare, and then when I woke up—"

He relaxed. "Just a dream, then." Kane forced a laugh. "Grace, I know it's tough not to know what happened, but just because you have a nightmare doesn't mean—"

"I *know* what happened. It was my fault. It was me."

He put his hands on her shoulders and gave her a soft

shake. "Nothing was your fault, Grace. You don't know what you're saying."

"I know exactly what I'm saying!" she cried, pushing him away. "I was driving!"

"Shut up!" he hissed, glancing around to make sure no one had heard. "You can't go around saying things like that," he told her softly, urgently. "You know they found drugs in your system. If people thought . . ." Did she not get how dangerous this was? Did she not understand what she was playing around with?

She rolled her eyes. "What's the difference? Everyone's going to know soon enough. The cops will make sure of that."

"The *cops*?" He grabbed her again, and this time, when she tried to push him away, he gripped tighter, pushing her up against the wall. "What did you do?"

"Nothing," she admitted. "Yet. But I have to tell them."

"Are you fucking insane?" He rubbed his fingers against the bridge of his nose, searching for a way to make her understand. "Whatever you think you remember, Grace, you've got to just forget about it. This isn't something to screw around with."

"I don't *think* I remember, Kane. I *know* what happened. And I know what you saw. I just don't know why you lied about it."

Join the club, Kane thought bitterly. It was his general policy not to get involved, and yet he'd opened his big mouth, spit out a single lie, and now it was too late. He was involved.

And, even more puzzling: He didn't completely regret it.

"Grace, listen to me, okay?" He leaned against the wall

next to her and stared off into the grayish morning haze. "I'm trying to help you, so you have to listen to me. You cannot talk to the cops. You'll ruin your life."

"So?" she muttered. "I ruined hers."

Kane pretended not to hear. "At least don't do anything yet," he insisted. "Just think about it. Give yourself some time. Don't be an idiot about this. It's too big."

"And why should I listen to you?" Her voice had lost its anger and was now just a flat, tired-sounding monotone.

Because I'm your friend, he wanted to tell her. *Because someone has to look out for you since you're doing such a shit job of it yourself.* "I know about getting into trouble," he said wryly. "And I know about getting *out* of it."

"Maybe I don't want to get out of it," Harper snapped, opening the emergency exit door and slipping back inside the school. "Maybe I just want what I deserve."

Beth shoved her fist against her mouth to stifle a scream. Then she bit down, hard, tears springing to her eyes—not from the pain.

Above her, she could hear Kane pacing back and forth on the landing, muttering to himself. She couldn't make out his words, but then, it didn't matter—she'd already heard enough. Beth tugged her knees to her chest and wrapped her arms around them tight, rocking back and forth, trying to drive the new knowledge out of her brain.

She'd cut class for the first time ever, needing to be alone. Kane had shown her the spot, long ago. That day, they had lounged on the landing, kissing in the sun. Today she had slunk down the rickety stairs and retreated to the dank, narrow space below. She had pressed herself up against the concrete retention wall, closed her eyes, and hoped, just for a few minutes, to hide from her life.

But the truth had found her.

Harper had been driving the car.

Harper had been drugged up, and Harper had gotten behind the wheel.

Kaia was dead. And Beth was to blame.

It was that simple.

Not my fault, she'd insisted, over and over again. The mantra had been a wall between her and an ocean of terror and guilt.

And now the wall had crumbled. And she was drowning. She couldn't think, couldn't move, couldn't do anything but rock back and forth as two words battered her brain.

My fault. My fault. My fault. Her lips moved, but no sound came out, not because she had no air left but because she was a coward. Kane was still up there. She could—*should*—stand up and scream out the truth about what she'd done, but the thought of moving made her dizzy. "Give yourself some time," Kane had told Harper, and it was as if he'd been talking to Beth.

And in a way, he had—he'd been talking to Kaia's killer.

Me.

She needed to slow down; she needed to think.

"Shit!" Kane's voice. There was a loud clang, as if he'd kicked the railing. Then the door opened, closed. And she was alone.

I killed her, Beth thought, testing the way the words sounded in her head. She almost laughed out loud; it sounded ridiculous. She'd never stolen anything, never gotten a speeding ticket, never been in a fight, still felt guilty when she lied to her parents. She was responsible, she was caring—she was *good*. And yet . . .

She squeezed her eyes shut and held her breath, willing herself to wake up and discover that the last month had been a stupid nightmare, that the box of pills was still sitting on her nightstand and Kaia was still alive. She would do anything, give up anything, to go backward. Maybe, if she wished for it hard enough, if she made enough silent promises, she could open her eyes and be back in January. None of this seemed real, anyway; maybe it wasn't.

She opened her eyes and she was still huddled on the ground, facing a blank wall. Nothing had changed.

It didn't matter what she'd meant to do, she told herself. All that mattered were the consequences.

You say you're a good person, she thought. *Prove it.*

Beth stood up, hyperconscious of every breath as if, without constant monitoring, she might forget to take another one. She trudged up the stairs and opened the door, squeezing the handle so tightly that it left an angry red slash across her palm. Now what? She would have to find Harper, or maybe the principal—or maybe she should just go directly to the police. She didn't know how these things worked, aside from the stray detail she'd picked up from *Law & Order*. Maybe she'd get to face off against Jesse Martin in the interrogation room. That wouldn't be so bad. Or Chris Noth. Except he was kind of old and bloated these days, and—

She almost burst into laughter again, and stopped herself just in time, fearing that once she started, she might never stop. She was losing it.

"Hey, watch it!"

Someone slammed past her as she stumbled blindly down the hall, and she suddenly realized that she was surrounded by people. The bell must have rung. She should be getting to her second-period class. She wouldn't want to get in trouble for being late—

The crazy laughter threatened to bubble up again, as she remembered herself. What was detention, compared to a jail sentence? What was facing down an angry teacher, compared to facing down the knowledge that she was a killer?

"Beth! Thank God I found you—" A short girl with dirty blond hair grabbed her and pulled her over toward the wall, out of the stream of students. It took a moment for Beth to register her identity: Hilary, the perky vice-chair of the Senior Spirit committee. "Listen, we have to talk; the auction this afternoon's going to be a total disaster if we don't figure this stuff out."

"What?" Beth asked weakly, backing away.

"The *auction*," Hilary repeated. "You missed the meeting yesterday, and we still need to get final approval on the list of participants and talk to Mr. Grady about—"

"I really . . . I really can't deal with this right now," Beth protested. "I've got to . . . I can't talk."

"Okay, okay, then let's pick a time to meet." Her words tumbled out at lightning speed, and Beth could barely follow her; or maybe Beth's mind was staging a slowdown. "I can't do third period because I have a test, but maybe I could get out of fourth if I got Grady to sign off on it or fifth period lunch—when are you free?"

"I don't . . ." Beth tried to battle her way through the

fog and come up with something coherent to say. She had a test next period, she realized, and a project to present in the next, and at lunch she was supposed to be assigning articles for the next edition of the *Gazette* and then doing an extra credit project for chem lab, and—and she gasped. Because all of that was irrelevant now. If she walked down the hall and into the principal's office and turned herself in, it wouldn't matter that she'd skipped her calculus test or ditched a newspaper meeting. She felt like she was living out two lives, or worse, was split between two levels of reality, and one was about to consume the other. She was about to lose everything, and the weight of what she'd done and what she needed to do pressed down on her like a vise, squeezing her chest until it felt like her organs would mash together and it would all finally stop.

"Beth? Are you okay? You look a little . . . pale."

The voice sounded like it was coming from a great distance. "I'm fine," Beth said, and her own voice sounded even farther away. She tried to say something else, but she couldn't breathe, much less speak. Hilary's concerned face slowly faded out of view as her field of vision turned to white, then gray, like poor TV reception breaking the world down into a blank screen of scrambled light. Beth felt her control slipping away and, along with it, her panic.

Maybe now I don't have to decide what happens next, she thought as her knees buckled and Hilary caught her just before her head smacked against the linoleum floor. Someone somewhere was shouting and footsteps were pounding and Beth didn't care about any of it anymore. She just closed her eyes and let it all fade away. *Maybe this is the end.*

✧✧✧

She might have made it out safely if her phone hadn't rung. Harper had persevered through the morning and made it to lunch—largely because her mother had driven her to school and she didn't have any way of getting home early that didn't involve throwing herself on someone's (read: Miranda's) mercy. But class was torture, as was lunch, a silent staring contest between Miranda and Harper, ensconced across the room from their usual table—the better to avoid Kane—neither commenting on the change or on much of anything beyond that night's history homework and the possibility of their gym teacher having another nervous breakdown.

By the time the bell rang, Harper had resolved to get out, somehow. She didn't want to drag Miranda along, as that would involve offering some kind of explanation— painful but true, or false but exhausting—and her leg still hurt too much to make the long walk home. But surely, if she could just sneak off campus, she could find a nice, quiet place to hide and wait for the day to officially end. Thanks to the senior auction, the end would come more quickly than usual, and her mother wouldn't think anything of it if Harper called home asking for an early pickup. (An even earlier pickup, courtesy of a never-fail headache-cramps-dizziness combo and a trip to the nurse's office, had crossed her mind, but she'd quickly vetoed it. These days, her mother would just drag her straight to the doctor for excessive testing and monitoring, a fate worse than school, if such a thing were possible.)

So she got rid of Miranda, tossed her uneaten lunch, and followed the crowd out of the cafeteria and down the hall, hoping to slip outside unnoticed. She had just stepped outside, smiling at the rush of cool air against her face, when her phone rang.

Harper cursed, knowing she shouldn't have turned it on after class, but she hadn't been able to resist.

Restricted number.

She didn't need caller ID to tell her it was Detective Wells—and if she just answered now and told the truth, all this would be over. But she couldn't do it. She stopped walking and slouched against the wall, staring at the flashing red light on the top of her phone; part of her wanted to throw it against the concrete pavement as hard as she could and watch it shatter, as if that would be the end of anything.

It was her own fault that she didn't hear him coming.

"Harper Grace? Is that you? What are you doing out here?"

Mr. Grady was a round little man with a rapid-fire smile and a walrus mustache who'd never forgotten the glory days of his high school drama career and now never missed the chance for a performance, onstage or off. Harper avoided him whenever possible.

She slipped the phone back into her bag, only half grateful that the decision, for the moment, had been made for her.

"Good lord, Harper, whatever has come over you, you look pale as a ghost!" Mr. Grady boomed, his voice tinged with a vaguely British, entirely fake accent that he claimed to have picked up during his "time abroad." (Harper and Miranda had always suspected he'd picked it up from one too many nights on the couch in front of *Masterpiece Theatre*.)

"Just getting some air," Harper said with a sigh, already resigned to her fate: school.

"Good, good," Mr. Grady said, bouncing up and down on the balls of his feet. "Always best to energize yourself before a performance, I always say. Now, you'll need a pass so you don't get in trouble for being late."

"Uh . . . performance?" She realized as soon as she said it that she should have just kept silent; he was already fumbling with a pad of hall passes, and she didn't want to endanger her Get Out of Detention Free card by pointing out that he was possibly insane, certainly mistaken.

"Well, perhaps not in the *technical* sense of the word," Mr. Grady admitted, winking at her, "but I won't tell if you won't. After all, people like you and I know that any public appearance is a performance, don't we?" He handed her the hall pass and then, before she could escape, placed a hand on her shoulder. "I have to admit, Harper, I'm surprised to see you getting back on the horse so quickly, after your rather . . . unfortunate turn at the podium last month. And to put yourself out there in the service of your fellow students? Magnificent, young lady, simply magnificent!"

At the thought of her "unfortunate turn," Harper almost gagged; she remembered little more than the glare of the spotlight, the murmurs of the audience, and the sense that everything was spiraling out of control. But the days before her speech were still clear in her mind, and they'd all been colored with an overwhelming fear of public speaking; for a million reasons, it wasn't an experience she was planning to repeat anytime soon.

"What are you talking about, Mr. Grady?" She pulled away from him; it was bad enough when anyone touched her, these days. But nothing skeeved her out more than the familiar well-meaning shoulder grip, usually deployed by middle-aged men barred—by decorum, circumstance, Harper's hostile glare, or their own awkwardness—from anything more openly affectionate. "How exactly am I serving my fellow students?"

"At this afternoon's auction, of course!" He tapped his clipboard. "I've got you down right here: dinner date with Harper Grace. Should go for a pretty penny, I'd wager, a popular girl like you."

"What?! No. No way. That's a mistake. I never signed up for—"

"Now, now, don't be nervous. It's a little late to back out now."

Her stomach churned, waiting for her to decide on an emotion—she was torn between fear (of having to go through with it) and loathing (for the demonic loser who'd signed her up). But neither of those would be of much help now. "Actually, Mr. Grady, I'm really going to have to—back out, I mean." She gave him a weak, brave smile and put her hand to her head. "I'm just not feeling very well, and actually, I was headed off to the nurse." Better to be fussed over by her mother and a team of hack doctors than to have to parade around on an auction block in front of the whole senior class, most of whom would undoubtedly be hoping—and waiting—for her to humiliate herself once again.

The sympathy ploy might have worked on some teachers, but the oblivious Grady was too intent on insuring that everything followed his script and the show went on. "Nonsense!" he cried, flinging his hands in the air. "Stage fright, preshow jitters, that's all. I've seen it a million times before. Nothing to worry about. This will do you good." He put one hand on each of her shoulders, squeezed tight, and steered her firmly back into the school. "I expect to see you backstage in an hour, Harper. *No excuses.* This is going to be just the medicine you need."

"But Mr. Grady—" she protested, cursing the pleading tone in her voice and wondering what had happened to the authoritative, autocratic Harper Grace who could have any teacher wrapped around her little finger in under ten minutes. Another by-product of her "unfortunate turn" at the podium, she supposed, and the "unfortunate" events that followed. The teachers all looked at her with pity now, and a bit of wariness; they *watched* her, as if last month's disaster had just been the beginning, and the full saga of destruction had yet to play out.

"I'd hate to have to give you detention for backing out on your responsibilities," he warned her in a jolly voice. "But I will, if need be. It's for your own good, after all. Now, now, nothing to be afraid of," he said, depositing her in front of her classroom. "As the bard says, 'All the world's a stage'! So really, we're all performing, all the time. Even now."

Thanks for the heads up, Harper thought bitterly. *Now tell me something I don't know.*

"I've got thirty, do I hear thirty-five?"

"Thirty-five!" a high, desperate voice shouted from the back.

Mr. Grady beamed and waved his gavel in the air. "That's thirty-five from the lovely lady in the back. Do I hear forty?"

"Forty!"

"Forty-five!"

"Fifty!"

"Fifty dollars!" Grady boomed. "We can do better than that." Silence from the crowd. "Let me remind you ladies that you're not just purchasing a lesson in driving a stick shift, you're purchasing the company of this handsome young man for one entire afternoon. Now that *must* be worth at least fifty-five dollars!"

It was worth twice that, Miranda thought, smiling at Kane's obvious discomfort up onstage as Mr. Grady whipped the crowd into a frenzy. But if even if she hadn't maxed out her allowance for the last few weeks, she wouldn't have allowed herself to place a bid. That was most definitely against the rules.

"Seventy-five dollars!" someone yelled. Miranda whipped around to her left and spotted Cheryl Sheppard, a ditzy brunette with a double-D chest and an even bigger wallet, waving her hand in the air.

"Seventy-five dollars!" Mr. Grady announced, fanning himself as if the bid had caused some kind of heat stroke. "Do I hear more?"

There were some murmured complaints from the crowd, but no one spoke up.

"Going once?"

"Going twice?"

Crack! Miranda jumped as the gavel slammed against the podium. "Sold, to the young woman in blue."

Kane grinned and gave Cheryl a cocky wave before strutting offstage. At least that solved the mystery of why he would have deigned to participate in this kind of thing to begin with. Kane was the opposite of a joiner; he was the guy that—at least in junior high—joiners used to run away from for fear of wedgies. But Miranda supposed that the chance to watch a room full of girls practically throw money at the stage just for the privilege of spending an afternoon with him had been too much to resist.

And she didn't care, she told herself. This was yet another example of why Kane was the last person she should waste her time thinking about—evidence, as if she needed any more, that just because he'd finally noticed her lips were good for more than snarky banter didn't mean he wanted anything more, or ever would. She should just smile and clap unenthusiastically, as she had after Lark Madison's brownie-baking lesson went for twenty bucks and Scott Pearson's old golf clubs went for fifty. *Pretend you care that your class is raising some money,* she reminded herself. *Pretend you don't care about* him.

"Now that you ladies have had your turn, it's time for the fellows to pull out your wallets, because next up, we have the beautiful Harper Grace."

Miranda almost choked.

Grady waved his hand toward the wings. Nothing happened. Nodding his head at someone behind the curtain, he beckoned frantically, then turned back to the audience. "As I was saying, the beautiful Harper Grace." Harper walked slowly and confidently toward the center of the stage, where she rejected his offer of a chair and stood with her hands on her hips, facing down the crowd. "She's auctioning off one dinner date, at the restaurant of your choice. Shall we start the bidding at thirty dollars?"

What the hell are you doing? Miranda asked silently,

wishing she could send her best friend—if that was even the name for it these days—a telepathic message. She willed Harper to seek her out in the crowd, hoping that, if they made some eye contact, Harper could give her some kind of sign that would explain how she'd ended up as the poster girl for Grady's manic auctioneering. But Harper wasn't making eye contact with her, or anyone. She'd fixed her eyes on a point in the back of the room, above the heads of the audience, and remained frozen, expression serene, mouth fixed in a Mona Lisa smile. She looked almost as if she wanted to be up there; which, Miranda supposed, must somehow be the case.

"Do I hear thirty dollars?"

Miranda suddenly realized that the auditorium was silent. Not just normal high school assembly quiet, where the air still buzzed with gossip and commentary, but the eerie, ominous *Who died?* quiet of the kind you find in lame horror movies, when the heroine puts her hand on the doorknob, just before it turns beneath her grasp and the spooky sound track kicks in.

"Okay . . . do I hear twenty-five dollars? Twenty-five dollars for a night on the town with Harper Grace?"

More silence. Miranda wanted to place a bid herself, just to end the misery, but that, obviously, would be the most humiliating blow of all. She kept her mouth shut. And onstage, Harper seemed barely aware of her surroundings or Grady's swiftly fading enthusiasm. She just smiled.

"Twenty-five dollars!" a nasal voice called out from the front row. Miranda didn't have to crane her neck to see the bidder; she would recognize Lester Lawrence's voice anywhere after sophomore year, when he'd called every

Tuesday night for three months, waiting for her to change her mind about a date and succumb to his well-hidden charms. Harper didn't even wince.

"Thirty dollars!" A Texan twang from the back, owned by Horace Wheeler, who also owned an extensive gun collection he was fond of exhibiting to creeped-out visitors who'd made the mistake of stopping by his parents' Wild West–themed ranch.

Out of the frying pan, into the firing range.

"I have thirty dollars," Grady said, feigning excitement. "Do I hear more? Going once? Going twice?" He was talking quickly, as if eager to end the awkwardness and move right along to the next victim.

"A hundred dollars!" someone shouted.

Harper flinched.

Oh, no. Miranda slumped down in her seat, shaking her head. He really was the dumbass of the year.

"A hundred dollars!" Grady repeated, a smile radiating across his face. "Going once? Going twice? Sold, to our very own basketball champion!"

Oh, Adam, she moaned silently. *You poor idiot.*

He'd just wasted a hundred dollars on what he probably thought was the ultimate chivalrous gesture, sweeping in to rescue Harper from her humiliation, saving the day as all heroes can't help but do. And he'd obviously failed to notice that the rest of the school would see it as nothing more than a hundred-dollar pity date, a fresh sign of just how far the mighty Harper had fallen.

Miranda knew how much Harper hated to be rescued; she knew better than most, since she'd been trying to do exactly that for a month now, to no avail. The harder you pushed, the faster Harper ran away, and poor, oblivious Adam had just guaranteed a record-breaking sprint.

Not that you'd know it from looking at her, of course. As Grady banged the gavel to a smattering of applause and a growing tide of laughter, Harper just gave the audience a curt nod, as if she'd done them all a favor by gracing them with her presence but was too polite to accept their gratitude. Then she turned on her heel and walked off toward the wings, where, Miranda knew, she would remain calm and dry-eyed, proud to the bitter end.

Miranda was the one who bent over in her seat, burying her head in her hands, ignoring the arrival of Inez Thompson onstage to auction off a painting from her father's gallery of cheesy desert-sunset paintings. Feeling like she'd been the one to stand up onstage weathering the silence, wishing that she could have been the one, or could at least have done something, *anything* to help, rather than, as always, remaining quiet and ineffectual in the face of Harper's pain, she squeezed her lips together against a wave of nausea.

This was how it always was in their friendship: Miranda waiting on the sidelines, while Harper fought the battles and reaped the rewards. It was better that way, Miranda had always told herself. Harper was the strong one, who could take anything, as she'd just proven to herself and everyone watching.

Miranda was the one who cringed at every blow, as if she were the one being struck. And when it was all over and Harper was left battered but still standing, Miranda was the one who cried.

✧✧✧

Beth woke up as someone laid a cool, damp washcloth across her head, but she didn't open her eyes. It was too easy just to lie there, on the small cot in the nurse's office, and let someone take care of her. The nurse's small radio was set to an easy-listening station, and the numbing sound of light jazz, punctuated only by occasional static or a soporific DJ, had lulled Beth to sleep shortly after the nurse laid her down for "a little R & R." She would have been happy to stay that way. But the cot was uncomfortable, the washcloth was dripping down her face, and eventually, as Beth shifted around, trying to force her body back to sleep, the nurse realized that her patient was finally awake.

"Feeling better, dear?" she asked, sounding significantly more sympathetic and nurselike than she had the last time Beth encountered her, trying to teach sex-ed to a horde of hormonally crazed teenagers. She seemed much more relaxed and competent here in her natural habitat. "Ready to sit up?"

Beth had only passed out for a few seconds, but when she awoke to find herself flat on her back in the middle of the hallway, twenty or thirty faces gawking down at her, the nurse had insisted on taking her down to the office. Beth wasn't about to resist; her mind was still sluggish and fuzzy, and she was happy to leave it that way for as long as possible.

They didn't trust her to drive herself home; probably for the best—she didn't trust herself. And she couldn't pull her parents out of work and make them lose a day's pay just because she couldn't handle her stress. She'd be burden enough, once they found out the truth. So the nurse had let her recuperate in her office for the rest of the day, and

Beth had stayed there, sleeping on and off, hiding out from her tests and her projects and her meetings and her decisions until the final bell rang, and it was time to escape.

"I'm feeling a lot better," she said truthfully. "Thanks for letting me hang out here."

"Are you sure?" The nurse frowned with concern. "I still think I should send you on to a doctor, have someone check you out."

"No, no, I'm fine," Beth protested. "I didn't eat anything this morning, and it just . . . got to me. Really. I feel okay now."

She had a job interview after school, one that might actually pay off, and she couldn't miss it, anxiety attack or not. *Except I don't need the job now, do I?* she asked herself. What would she do with spending money in reform school? Or prison?

But she forced herself to stop thinking about what she'd heard that morning, and what she was going to do about it. She needed to be rational and plan her next move, and to do that, she had to make it through the rest of the day. Tonight, she promised herself, she would figure everything out. She would find a way to live with herself—she would have to.

Beth waved off the nurse's concerns and gathered her stuff, then, steeling herself, rejoined the outside world. Managing to make it down to the parking lot without speaking to anyone—not too difficult, considering that she'd run out of friends weeks ago and so only needed to dodge the handful of acquaintances who needed something from her—she got into her car and wrapped her hands around the wheel.

I could crash too, she told herself. *I could pull out onto the road and crash into anything. No drugs, just me. Just an accident. It could happen to anyone.*

But it was no comfort; yes, some deaths were random, some accidents were really just that. But some effects had causes—some victims had killers.

"Stop," she ordered herself again, aloud in the empty car. She couldn't think about it while she was driving, not unless she really did want to crash into something. (And she didn't, she assured herself. Much as she hated herself and what she'd done, it would never come to that.)

By the time she'd pulled into the lot of Guido's Pizza, she'd reassembled herself into some semblance of calm. She smoothed down her hair and did a quick mirror check: She wasn't exactly decked out in a suit and heels for her interview, but then, given Guido's usual T-shirt and grease-smeared apron, her faux cashmere and khakis would probably do the job.

Just keep it together, she begged herself. *Just for one more hour, keep it together.*

And she did, all the way across the parking lot, up to the door of the restaurant, where she almost slammed into a guy backing out the door carrying a large stack of pizza boxes.

He turned around to apologize—and she nearly lost it.

"Hey," Reed said, his smile just peeking out over the top of the boxes.

"Hey." Her heart slammed against her chest. Would he be able to tell, just by looking at her? she wondered. Was her guilt painted across her face?

"Listen, about yesterday . . ."

"I've gotta go," Beth said quickly, clenching her stomach and trying to keep her lower lip from trembling. She brushed past him and stepped inside, immediately blasted by a wave of garlic that made her want to throw up.

"See you later?" he called hopefully as the door shut behind her.

Beth pressed both hands to her face and took a deep breath. *God, I hope not.*

chapter

6

It turned out that "Guido" was actually Roy, a sixty-two-year-old widower from Vegas who, having a hankering for small-town life, had moved west to find himself. He'd found Grace instead, a go-nowhere, do-nothing town in dire need of a pizza parlor, however mediocre.

And that's pretty much all Beth took in from his half-hour monologue as she trembled in the chair across from him, willing him to continue talking so that she wouldn't have to speak. It was hard enough to listen when there were so many loud thoughts crowding into her head.

"My daughter, she wanted me to move in with her and her husband. They fixed up the room over the garage real nice."

My life is over.

"I raised her right—but that's no life for a man, livin' off his daughter, wasting away the days starin' at someone else's walls."

My life should *be over. I killed her.*

"It'd be different if there were grandkids, but you know how it is today, no one's got any time for family. 'What's the hurry, Dad?' she keeps asking me. 'What are you waiting for?' I say, but she just laughs, and that husband of hers . . . it's not my place to say, but if you ask me, he doesn't want the bother."

I didn't mean to.

"He's not a worker, that one. Never did a day's hard work in his life. Not like me. Twenty-five years at the casino and now here I am, shoveling the pizzas every day, and let me tell you, life couldn't get much better."

But it's still my fault.

"Couldn't get much worse, either, if you know what I mean. That's life, eh? Gotta take that shit and turn it into gold, I always say. And it's not so bad. Rent's low, sun's always shining, and customers know better than to talk back."

Ruining my life won't change anything.

"'Course, can't say as I don't miss the old days. Vegas now? That's nothin' but a theme park. But in my day . . . yeah, you had your mob, and you had your corruption— but you also had your strippers and your showgirls and your cocktail waitresses. And then there was my Molly. . . ."

I don't even know what really *happened.*

"So what's your story? I got your résumé here, and I see you got plenty of experience serving. But why ditch the cushy diner job and come here? Don't know as I'd see this place as a step up."

I know what happened.

"Beth? You still with me?"

Beth tuned back in to realize that a large, calloused hand was waving in front of her face. "Oh . . . sorry. Yes."

"So?"

She tucked her hair behind her ears, a nervous habit. "So . . . I'm, uh . . ." She wasn't good at bluffing, even on a good day. And this had not been a good day. "I didn't quite hear what you asked."

He gave her a friendly smile. "Nerves got you, eh? Take your time. A few deep breaths never hurt anyone."

She tried to follow his suggestion, but the heavy scent of garlic made her head pound. She didn't know why he was being so nice to her. She didn't know why *anyone* would be nice to her anymore.

"I asked why you wanted this job," he repeated.

But Beth couldn't concentrate on sounding responsible or eager to work in a grease-stained pit. She just shrugged. "I think it would be . . . I mean, I like pizza, and . . ." She'd prepared a perfect answer the night before—but it had escaped from her mind, and now she had nothing. She held her hands out in surrender. "I need the money."

He grinned. "Who doesn't? And why'd you leave your last job?"

Another perfect answer that she no longer had. "Creative differences?" she said instead, giving Roy a hopeful smile.

"Gonna have to ask you to be more specific on that one, hon."

"Well . . ." She giggled nervously, her eyes tearing up. "I dumped a milk shake on one of the customers."

"Can't say as clumsiness is something I look for in a waitress," he said, tipping his head to the side. "But I'm no ballerina myself, if you know what I mean."

"No," she said quickly. "No, I did it on purpose. I just

dumped it on his head. It felt great." Her giggles grew into full-scale laughter, the kind that steals control of your limbs and your better judgment. There was no joy in the spasms rocketing through her body, just an explosion of all the tension she'd been storing since morning—once it started coming out, she couldn't figure out how to shove it back in again. She flopped around on the chair, heaving with hysteria, gasping for breath, until finally Roy's frozen scowl brought her back to reality.

"Look, I don't know what the joke is," he said, standing up, "but I really don't have time for this kind of thing."

"No!" she cried, leaping up. "No joke. This isn't me— I'm a great employee, really, just give me another chance, I really need this job, I've tried everywhere else in town—"

His expression warmed, but he shook his head. "I'm sorry. I am. But I can't hire you just because I feel bad for you—I need someone reliable, and it's pretty clear that you're—"

"Not," she finished for him. It would have been hilarious if it hadn't been so sad. Reliable was all she'd ever been. Good ol' reliable Beth. And now she didn't even have that. She slumped down over the table, her head resting on her arms and her arms resting on something wet and sticky, but she didn't cry. She'd been holding it all in for hours now, and it seemed the tears had all dried up.

When she felt the hand on her shoulder, she knew who it was, and she knew she should stand up and rush out of the restaurant without even looking at him, but she was too weak and too selfish, and so she lifted her head up and smiled. "Hey. Again."

"You're having a bad week," Reed said, without a

question in his voice. "Come on." He grabbed her arm gently and pulled her out of the chair, walking her toward the door. She let herself go limp, happy for a moment to be a marionette and let someone else pull the strings.

Once outside, he sat her down on the bumper of his truck, then perched up on the hood.

"I should go," she mumbled, avoiding eye contact. "I should get out of here."

"Slow down." He pulled something out of his pocket—a small, squished paper tube, and offered it to her. "This always helps," he explained.

Drugs, she thought, and the hysterical laughter threatened to burble out of her again. *Why does every guy I'm with keep shoving drugs in my face? Doesn't he know what could happen?* That shut down the laughter impulse immediately; Reed, better than anyone, knew what could happen. She waved the joint away and sighed heavily.

"What is it?" he asked, his soft, concerned voice so incongruous against his punk rock wardrobe and apathetic pose. "What's going on?"

"Nothing. I just screwed up my interview," she admitted. "And everything."

Reed laughed, a slow, honeyed chuckle. "Don't worry about 'Guido.' He's a pushover. I'll talk to him, vouch for you—he listens to me."

"Why bother?" she asked. "You don't even know me."

"So tell me."

"What?"

"About you."

So she told him about how she made up stories for

her little brothers when they had trouble falling asleep, and about the stacks of blank journals that were piled up on her bookshelf, each with two or three entries she'd written before getting distracted and giving up. He told her that he'd taught himself to play the guitar when he was twelve, when the school had started using the music room for detention overflow. She admitted that she liked Natalie Merchant, Tori Amos, Dar Williams—the sappier, the better. He admitted that he hated the whole girl-power, singer-songwriter, release-your-inner-woman genre, but recommended Fiona Apple and Liz Phair to bulk up her collection.

They didn't talk about Kaia.

Reed was lying back on the hood of the truck, staring up at the darkening sky. Beth couldn't stop watching him, the way he moved his body with such fluid carelessness, as if he didn't care where it ended up. The cuffs of his jeans were fraying, and his sockless ankles peeked out above his scuffed black sneakers. Beth resisted the crazy urge to touch them.

"I should take off," she said, realizing that the sky was fully dark—her brother's babysitter would be eager to leave, and her parents would be expecting to find dinner on the table when they got home from work.

"Wait—" He grabbed her wrist, and she gasped as the touch sent a chill racing up her arm. Their eyes locked, and neither of them spoke for a long moment. She had time to notice that his skin was softer than she'd expected, and then, abruptly, he pulled away. "If you need me . . ." He dug a scrap of paper and a stubby pencil out of his back pocket. She now knew he always kept one on hand, for times when a strain of melody popped into his head and he needed to record it before it disappeared. He scrawled down a number and handed it to her.

Beth knew she shouldn't take it; she should never have allowed herself to lean on Reed, even for an afternoon. But she let him hand it to her, and she let herself smile when their fingers touched.

"Why are you doing this?" she asked.

"What?"

"Being so . . . *nice.*"

"Because you—" He stopped in the middle of a word, closed his mouth, and looked beyond her for a moment, out to the dark horizon beyond Guido's pizza shack. She wondered if he was thinking about that day on the side of the highway—and she wondered if letting him believe in it, and believe in her, counted as a lie. "Because you look like you could use it."

She couldn't stand it anymore. "Reed, I should tell you—"

"I gotta go." He gave her an awkward wave before sliding into the driver's seat.

"Wait—"

But before she could say anything more, he shut the door and drove away.

"A little to the left, farther, no, now to the right, faster, faster, okay . . . not there—now! That's it! *Yes!*"

"Awesome!" Miranda cried, tossing down the controller and shooting her fists in the air. "I rock!"

"You really do," Adam marveled. He threw himself

back on the couch, kicking his feet up on the coffee table. "Who knew?"

"High score!" Miranda cheered, pointing at the screen. "See that? I got the high score."

"Mmph," Adam grunted.

"Oh, don't get cranky just because you got beat by a girl." Miranda tapped her thumb against the buttons until her initials were correctly entered in as a testament to her glory. "Where has this game been all my life?" She glanced over at Adam, giving him a playful grin. "Think I could convince the phys ed department to give me some sort of credit for playing Wild Taxi?"

"*Crazy* Taxi," Adam corrected her. "You've really never played before?"

Miranda shook her head. "My cousin gave me his old PlayStation, but that was, like, when I was a kid. And it broke after a couple days. This is much cooler."

"Okay, so what's next? Resident Evil or Tony Hawk?"

Miranda checked her watch and her eyes bugged out. "Adam, we've been playing for *two hours*." She hadn't even noticed the time passing, which was pretty much a miracle since the first ten minutes in Adam's living room had dragged on forever. Without Harper around, the two had nothing to say to each other; all the more reason to consider Sega Dreamcast a gift from the gods.

"Yeah? So?" Adam hopped off the couch. "Hungry? I could order a pizza, and I think we've got some chips or something—"

"Adam, we haven't even started looking at math," she pointed out. "What about your test?"

"What about *your* high score?" he countered. "You

really gonna leave it undefended and let me kick your ass?" He plopped down on the floor beside her, lifting a controller and restarting the game.

"But . . ." Miranda stopped. If he didn't want to work, it was his funeral, right, she told herself. And after all, just one more game wouldn't hurt. . . .

They spent another hour glued to the screen, switching from Crazy Taxi to Tony Hawk to NBA 2K1 before they were interrupted again.

"No fair!" she yelled as he sank yet another three-pointer. "You're captain of the basketball team and I'm barely five feet tall—how am I supposed to block your shots?"

"Miranda, it's a video game," he reminded her. "Your guy's about seven feet tall and he was last year's MVP. I think it's a pretty fair matchup."

She was about to confess that she didn't actually understand the rules of basketball—a fatal weakness no matter how many all-stars her cyber-team was fielding—when her phone rang. She paused the game and checked the caller ID. Harper.

Adam caught the name on the screen and gave her a pained nod. "You take it. I'll practice my free throws."

Miranda flipped open the phone. "Hey, what's up?" she asked, pretending it was no big deal that Harper had called, though Harper *never* called, not anymore.

"Nothing. I just . . . can you talk?"

"Of course."

"What are you doing?"

"Nothing much. Just hanging out." It wasn't really a lie, Miranda told herself. And it was for a good cause—if she admitted she was busy, Harper would probably just use it as an excuse to hang up again. And if she admitted she was at Adam's house, fraternizing with the enemy . . . she'd have to explain what she was doing there, and Adam had asked her to keep that quiet and, all in all, it was easier just to be vague. "How about you?"

"Thinking."

"You?" Miranda asked, automatically slipping into sarcasm before she remembered that the old days were over.

But Harper laughed. "Crazy, I know. I need to ask you something. Do you think—"

"Woo hoo! High score, baby!"

Miranda winced as Adam's shouts echoed through the empty house.

"What was that?" Harper asked.

"What?" Miranda said. "I didn't say anything."

"The champion returns!"

"Is that Adam?" Harper asked, continuing on before Miranda had a chance to answer. "It is. What's Adam doing there?"

Miranda sighed. It would have been easier to ignore the whole thing, but she wasn't about to lie now, no matter what Adam had asked of her. It's not like he had anything to be embarrassed about—it was just Harper. "Actually, I'm at his house," she admitted.

Harper didn't say anything, and for a moment Miranda worried that the line had gone dead.

"Hello? Harper?"

"You're next door," she finally said in a low monotone. She didn't ask why.

Miranda laughed nervously. "It's not like we're hanging out, like we're friends or something. I have to be here—I mean, I don't *have* to, like it's some horrible ordeal. Actually, when you called, he was teaching me how to play some video game, which actually turned out to be fun—crazy, huh?"

"Wild."

She was babbling, the words spilling out before she had time to think better of it. Which was ridiculous, because there was no need to be nervous—it's not like she had snuck over here behind Harper's back. Yes, she'd walked thirty minutes instead of driving over, but not because she didn't want Harper to spot her car, she reasoned. It was just a beautiful day, and she needed the exercise, and . . . it's not like everything she did had to do with Harper, she insisted silently.

It's not like Harper had any right to care.

"But, really, we're supposed to be studying," she tried again. "See, Adam—"

"Miranda."

She stopped talking abruptly, as if Harper had flipped a switch.

"I don't want to hear it," Harper continued. "What do I care if the two of you want to hang out?"

"But we're not hanging out, I'm—"

"I don't want to bother you," Harper said loudly, talking over her. "Sorry I called. Talk to you later."

"Score!" Adam cried from the living room, just as the phone went dead. Miranda flipped it shut and pressed it against her forehead. However irrational it may have been, she felt like that was her one chance to fix things—and she'd blown it.

Reed hadn't set out with a destination in mind; he'd just wanted to take the edge off his strangely unsettled mood.

He felt like he'd forgotten something important, but his thoughts were too jumbled to pin down what it was. So he decided to ignore it and take a drive. He wasn't too surprised to see where he'd ended up. He made a sharp right and pulled off onto the small access road that led straight to the glass monstrosity. He'd always hated this house, with its jutting corners and its smooth, shiny facade. It looked like a machine, some gruesome futuristic gadget blown up to unnatural size and dropped into the middle of the desert. It looked *wrong*, its sleek silver lines out of place in the rolling beiges of the desert landscape.

Kaia had always complained about the scenery—or, as she was quick to point out, lack thereof. They'd stood on her deck and looked out at the deserted space surrounding her house and she'd seen nothing but an ocean of beige. She'd called it a wasteland, but only because she didn't see that what was sparse and clean could also be beautiful, precisely because it had nothing to hide. He hadn't had the words to explain it to her, however, so he'd just shrugged, and then kissed her.

She hated the house, too, but for different reasons. It was her outpost of civilization, true, but it was also her prison, and she resented its cream-colored walls and architecturally avant-garde floor plan, and even its size. She'd explained to him that her mother's penthouse apartment back home could fit into one wing of her father's mansion, and that the giant empty house swallowed her up and made her feel small and alone. It was the same way Reed felt about the desert, except he liked it.

Now the house really was empty. The windows had been dark and the driveway empty for weeks, until one day, Reed arrived to discover that the windows had been boarded up and a large FOR SALE sign planted in the absurdly well-manicured front lawn. But Reed kept coming back. He didn't have anything left of Kaia except his swiftly fading memories. He dreaded the day he forgot how her pale cheeks reddened when she laughed, or the hoarse sound in her voice when she'd just woken up; the house helped him remember.

"Don't I get some?" Kaia asks, grabbing his hand before he can bring the joint to his lips.

"You don't smoke," Reed reminds her.

"I know," she says, snatching it away and tossing it to the ground. "And neither should you. It makes you sound like an idiot."

"Doesn't take much," he mutters.

"Shut up."

"What?"

"Clueless smile?" She grazes her fingers across his lips. "Hot. Self-deprecation? Not."

They are lying on a blanket in front of the old Grace mines. It has become "their place," a phrase neither of them will say out loud because, as Kaia often points out, this is not 1957 and they are not teenyboppers in love. But nonetheless, it is their place; ever since Reed brought her here for the first time, he has been unable to think of it as anything else. He has been coming here since he was a kid, biking out along the deserted stretch of highway long before he had his driver's license, enjoying the sense of freedom and power that came from getting away from the safe and the familiar and getting by on his own. But now when he comes on his own, as he still does, something feels off. The cavernous warehouses, the decaying machinery, and the welcome darkness of the mines themselves are no longer enough. He misses Kaia; it has been only a couple weeks since they toppled to the happier side of the love-hate fence, but already he has gotten used to having her around.

Today they skipped school and drove out here instead. They lay next to each other, staring up at the sky, swapping the occasional insult and listening to each other breathe. He doesn't know what he's doing with her—rich, stuck-up, spoiled, beautiful. And she's made it clear that she doesn't know what she's doing with him. Neither of them care.

"Don't try to reform me," he warns her. "It won't take."

She rolls over onto her side, propping herself up to look at him. Her fingers toy with the curls falling over his forehead, and a smile plays at the corners of her lip. "Don't worry," she assures him. "You're good just the way you are."

"And how's that?"

"Hmmm . . . dirty." She rubs his chest, where a long, dark grease stain stretches across his shirt. "Smelly." She buries her face in his neck and breathes in deeply. "Grungy." She pulls his hands toward her face and kisses the tips of his fingers, ignoring the dirt lodged under each nail. "Mine."

He grabs her around the waist and rolls her over on top of him, lifting his head up to meet her lips. They kiss with their eyes open, and he can see himself reflected in her pupils. Her weight flattens him against the ground and he lets his head fall back as she spreads his arms out and entwines her fingers in his.

They stop kissing after only a few minutes, but she continues to lie on him, resting her head on his chest.

"Happy?" he asks, because he knows she never is.

"Shhh. I'm listening."

"To what?"

"Your heartbeat," she whispers. They are both still. Then she laughs. "Did I just say that? What the hell are you doing to me?"

She sighs and tries to roll off of him, but he wraps his arms around her and holds her in place.

"Turning you into a sap," he teases. "I like it."

"Don't try to reform me," she tells him. "It won't take."

"Don't worry," he says, echoing her words as she echoed his. "You're good just the way you are."

Too late, he forgets how she hates compliments from him, even in jest.

"It's getting cold," she says, and he can feel her muscles tense. "I'm getting out of here."

"Don't," he tells her. "Stay."

She breathes deeply, and as her chest expands, it pushes against his, forcing their breathing to fall into the same rhythm. "I don't know what we're doing here," she says, touching the side of his face.

"Who cares?" he asks, laying his hand over hers. "Don't go."

She kisses him, hard, her tongue prying his lips open and slipping in, her hands gathering the light cotton blanket into tight fists. This time she closes her eyes, but he keeps his open. He can't stop watching her, as if part of him harbors the childlike belief that if he closes his eyes, she might actually disappear.

He looked up at the sound of a siren—it blipped once, like a horn blast, as if to alert him that he was totally screwed, without waking the neighbors. (Not that there were any.) The flashing lights of the approaching car cast a yellowish-orange tinge over everything as Reed scrambled to stow his pot deep in the glove compartment and popped a breath mint, not that it would be of much help. Everything about him reeked of stoner, and even though he'd had his last joint an hour or two ago and was as alert as he ever got these days, if the cops wanted to bust him, they would. It's not like they hadn't done it before.

The car pulled onto the shoulder just behind his, and a figure stepped out. As he approached, Reed was surprised to note that it wasn't Sal or Eddie, the two beat cops who loved nothing more than handing out parking tickets and hassling "street punks," aka anyone under the age of eighteen who didn't dress like they were auditioning for an Abercrombie ad. Sal and Eddie had, until recently, been actual street punks—or, as close as Grace got to urban blight—until their shoplifting had gotten them banned from pretty much every store on Main Street and a number of drunken brawls had had the same effect on their barhopping days. They'd joined the police force for the thrill of running red lights; the guns were just a bonus.

This cop, an overweight guy in his mid-forties with a mustache and an eye-twitch, tapped on Reed's window. "Whatever you're up to, forget about it," he snapped, once Reed had rolled the window down. "Just get out of here."

That wasn't a cop uniform, Reed suddenly realized. It was gray, not navy blue, and a narrow label above the shirt pocket read CAPSTONE SECURITY. "What's it to you?" he asked. Sucking up to authority figures was bad enough; sucking up to a paunchy rent-a-cop who probably had a stash of his own hidden in the cruiser next to his mail-ordered Taser gun? Not gonna happen.

"Gimme a break, kid." The guy leaned against the truck, casually letting his jacket fall open to reveal the holster strapped underneath. It wasn't holding a Taser gun. "You think I'm out here in Crapville, USA, for my health?

They pay plenty to run punks like you off the property—so I'm telling you. Get."

"No one lives here anymore," Reed pointed out.

"Don't mean no one owns it." He glanced up at the deserted mansion and scowled. "And the guy who does is plenty pissed off. There've been some break-ins—but I don't suppose you'd know anything about that, eh?"

Reed just stared blankly at him.

"Yeah. Of course not. But now I'm here, and I've got my instructions."

"Yeah?"

"No lurkers. No prowlers. No squatters. No punks." He squinted into the truck and stared pointedly at a glass pipe that had rolled onto the floor. "I don't care which one you are. Just get going and don't come back."

"Or what?" Reed asked, something in him spoiling for a fight. "You'll call in the *real* cops?"

"Don't need 'em," the guy said, ambling away from the window. But he didn't head back to his car—instead, he circled the front of the truck and, looking up to give Reed a jaunty grin, smashed in the front headlight.

"Dude! What the hell are you doing?"

"Take my advice, kid. Just get out of here," the guy yelled, waving with his arm still and his fingers glued together in the universal sign for *buh-bye*. "Just drive away and don't look back."

"Harper, can you come down here for a second?" Her mother's normally lilting voice had a steely undertone that suggested her options were limited.

"Great, more family together time," Harper muttered,

burned out on bonding after a night that had already included ice-cream sundaes and four rounds of Boggle. Ever since the accident her parents had gone into maximum overdrive on the TLC front—failing to realize that, to Harper, tender loving care involved a few drinks, a sugar high, and plenty of uninterrupted alone time. Tonight the plan had been simple: barricade herself in her room, blast some Belle and Sebastian, bury her head under a pillow, and try to plan out her next step. She'd been a master strategist, once, and though it seemed like too long ago to remember, she was certain the skills had just gone into hibernation, waiting for a more hospitable climate before they re-emerged to save her. Family fun time didn't fit into her schedule.

"What?" she grunted as she trudged down the stairs. She stopped, midway down, catching sight of Kane's smooth hair and smoother style. He gave her a reptilian grin, then offered her parents a far warmer expression, compassion oozing from every orifice.

"It's just so good to see her up and around again," he told her parents, as if she weren't even in the room.

"Yes, *she's* thrilled to pieces," Harper said dryly. "What the hell do you want?"

"Harper!" Her mother shot her a scandalized look. Much as Harper despised the depths to which her family had sunk over the generations, from American-style royalty (read: outrageously wealthy with an attitude to match) to middle-middle-class plodders carrying the torch of small-town mediocrity, Amanda Grace hated it more. So much so that she refused to acknowledge that the family she'd married into no longer guarded the flame of civility amongst the heathens of the wild west. "People look to us," she'd often told a young Harper, lost in delusions of mannered grandeur, "and it's important we live up to expectations." Miss Manners had nothing on Amanda Grace; Emily Post would have been booted from the house for rude behavior. And a solicitous attitude toward guests, from visiting dignitaries (in her dreams) to collection agencies (a walking, and frequent, nightmare) was rule number one. Apparently even in her fragile, post-invalid state, Harper was still expected to abide by the Grace code of etiquette.

"As I was saying, Kane, it's so lovely of you to drop by," her mother said, placing a deceptively firm hand on Harper's shoulder. "*Isn't* it?"

"Lovely," Harper echoed. Her mother got a dutiful smile; Kane got the death glare.

"How are you feeling, sweetie?" her mother asked, releasing her grip.

"Fine." Harper scowled; if only everyone would stop asking her that a hundred times a day, maybe she'd actually have a prayer of it being true. Though that was doubtful, she conceded. How fine could she be when the most important moment of her life was lost in some fog of forgetfulness and the only glimpses her memory chose to grant her were the ones that proved she probably didn't deserve to live?

"That's great!" Amanda Grace turned to Kane. "I think it's a fine idea, then, as long as you don't have her out too late."

"Excuse me?" Harper snapped. "Could everyone stop talking about me like I'm invisible and—" She caught sight of her mother's face and forced herself to soften her tone. "What's a fine idea, *Kane*?"

"Well, *Harper*—" He winked at her, acknowledgment of the fact that he almost never used her first name and its appearance only confirmed that everything following would be a show put on for the sake of her parents. "I was just telling your parents that I thought you might enjoy it if I took you out for some coffee—"

"Decaf," her father interjected.

"Right, of course, decaf." Kane shrugged and gave everyone an "Aw shucks, aren't I a heck of a guy" look. "You've been cooped up in the house for so long, and we get so little chance to catch up in school, that I thought it might be nice. As long as your parents are okay with it, of course."

"It's quite refreshing," her father said, beaming. "Most of the time, you kids just dash off to some place or another and no one knows what the hell"—this time her father was the one who drew the patented Amanda glare—"I mean, heck, you're up to. I hope you know what a good friend you've got here, Harp. I think this one's a keeper."

"Oh, don't worry, I know exactly what I've got here," Harper said through gritted teeth. *Nice job with the Eddie Haskell impression,* she thought. *I'm suffocating in smarm.* Kane always boasted he could read minds—let him read that.

"I'm kind of tired, actually," she said, faking a yawn. "I was thinking I'd just stay here tonight . . ."

"You're spending too much time up in your room," her mother said, and behind the polite facade Harper could read real concern in her voice. "It'll be good for you to get out. Get back to—"

"Okay. Okay, fine, whatever," Harper cut in, knowing

that if one more person suggested that things could ever be normal again, she might spit, or scream, or simply collapse, any one of which was definitely a Grace etiquette *don't*. With a sigh, she slipped into a pair of green flip-flops and grabbed a faded gray hoodie from the closet. Her mother hated it—so much the better.

"Now, remember, don't be back too late," Amanda Grace reminded them as Kane escorted her out, hands tightly gripping her arm and waist.

"So now you're kidnapping me?" Harper asked, as soon as they were safely in the car. "General havoc and mischief making getting too boring for you, so you're moving on to felonies?"

"I don't know what you're talking about," Kane said, in his parent-proof, silky smooth voice. "I just wanted to spend some time with my good friend Harper, who's so recently been having such a tough time of it." There was a pause, then, *"Oof!"*

Kane talked tough, but shove a sharp elbow into his gut and he'd fold like a poker player with no face cards.

"What the hell was that for?" he asked, rubbing his side and giving her a wounded look. "You know I bruise easily."

"Gosh, I'm awfully sorry," Harper whined, pouring on some false solicitation of her own. "Whatever was I thinking?" Then she whacked him in the chest. "What the hell were you thinking? Since when do you ask my parents for my hand in coffee?"

"If I called and asked if you wanted to go out tonight, what would you have said?"

"You're assuming I would have picked up the phone?"

"Exactly," he concluded in an irritatingly reasonable voice. "You would have made the wrong choice. *Again*. So this time, I decided not to give you one."

"Fine." Harper leaned back against the seat and rolled her eyes toward the ceiling. "So where are you taking me? Bourquin's, at least? I can't drink that shit coffee they have at the diner."

He shook his head. "Guess again."

"*So* not in the mood for games, Kane. And you know exactly why."

"This isn't a game, Grace—you're the one who hasn't figured that out yet. You'll see where we're going soon enough."

She crossed her arms and turned toward the window. "Fine."

"Fine."

They drove in silence for several minutes. The radio might at least have lightened things up or offered them something neutral to argue about, but Kane made no move to switch it on and Harper wasn't about to do anything that might signify her willing participation in this ridiculous adventure.

They swung into a small parking lot and Kane turned off the car. "We're here."

"And where is . . . oh." They had pulled up in front of a large, boxy building, its face a windowless wall of institutional gray. A single door, also gray, stood square in the middle, and over it hung a neon blue-and-white sign that would have been enough to scare away most visitors if the decor hadn't already done the job: POLICE.

"What the hell is this, Kane?" Harper's eyes flicked

toward her bag, half expecting her phone to ring as if Detective Wells, who'd already left four or five messages for her over the course of the day, could somehow sense that she was nearby. Maybe she wouldn't bother to call—Harper turned back to the window, gaze fixed on the solid-looking door, wondering if it would swing open. Who would they send out to escort her inside, where she belonged? "Why would you bring me here?"

Kane shrugged, but this time there was nothing *aw-shucks* about it. "You're the one who said you wanted to talk to the cops. I thought I'd help you out. You want to confess your sins? You want to ruin your life? Go ahead."

"This isn't how it works," she retorted, struggling against encroaching panic. "This isn't—what do you want me to do, just march in there and say, 'Hey, just FYI, I was the one driving the car'?"

"You don't think they'd be interested to hear it?"

"This is what you want me to do?" Harper asked, her hand gripping the door handle.

"Isn't it what *you* want to do?" Kane sneered.

"It's the right thing. . . ."

"Absolutely. So go ahead."

"I'm just not . . ."

"No time like the present, Grace." Kane opened his own door—and at the sound of the latch releasing and the outside air rushing in, Harper almost gasped. "I'll go with you, if you want. Should be quite a show."

She couldn't say anything; she didn't move.

"What are you waiting for? They're right inside, just—"

"Stop!" she shouted, slapping her hand over her eyes so he wouldn't see the tears. "Why are you doing this?"

He slammed the door. "Why are *you* doing this?" he shouted, and it was the first time she could remember ever hearing him raise his voice. "What the hell are you trying to do to yourself?"

"What do you care?" she mumbled, still hiding her face.

"This is real, Harper. Look out there." When she didn't move, he grabbed her hands roughly and pulled them away from her eyes, jerking her head toward the police station. "*Look.* This isn't *Law & Order.* This is your life."

"It was her life, too," Harper said, almost too softly to hear.

"You don't know what happened," Kane said in an almost bored voice, as if he'd gotten tired of ticking off the items on the list. He'd stopped shouting and had released his grip on Harper's wrists, and was now staring straight ahead, his hands loosely resting on the wheel. "You don't remember anything about the accident—" She tried to interrupt, but he talked over her. "*Except* a few things you *think* you remember but could just be part of some Vicodin-induced nightmare."

"Percodan," she corrected him.

"Whatever. Okay, so you were driving. So what? There were drugs in your system—you don't know how they got there. You were going somewhere—you don't know where. Kaia's fingerprints were found all over that perv's apartment after he turned up with his head beat in—you don't know why. Another car forced you off the road— you don't know who. You don't know *anything* except that if you tell them you were behind that wheel, they'll crucify you."

"I know it's my fault," she said stubbornly.

"You don't know *anything*," he repeated loudly, over-enunciating each syllable.

And I can't stand it, she admitted, but only to herself.

"I'm not saying we can't figure it out," he suggested, turning toward her and slinging his arm across the back of her seat. "Do some investigating, poke around—you and me against the world, like the good old days?"

"So this isn't *Law & Order,* but now you want me to go all Veronica Mars on you?" Harper asked wryly.

"That's kind of a chick show." Kane smirked. "I was thinking more *CSI.* Or *Scooby-Doo* . . . you'd look pretty smoking in that purple dress, and I don't know"—he peered at himself in the rearview mirror—"think I could pull off an ascot?"

"This isn't funny," she said dully.

"I'm serious, Grace—if you want to know what happened, we can figure it out. *They* can't," he added, pointing toward the station. "They won't need to, because they'll have you. But we can fix things, and get them back to normal."

"Take me home," she told him, not wanting to think any more about the accident, or any of it.

He ignored her. "Start with the drugs—that's the key. Are you sure you didn't take *anything*?"

She remembered Kaia handing her two white pills: Xanax. She remembered popping them into her mouth and stepping onstage, and her world falling apart. But that couldn't be right.

"Take me home," she insisted, louder.

"Promise me you won't go to the cops," he retorted.

"I still don't get why you care."

"You don't have to," he said, looking away. "Just promise."

She had already promised herself that she would do the right thing; tonight was supposed to have been about figuring out what that was. Kane was the last person to go to for that kind of help. *On the other hand,* she thought, torn between horror and bemusement, *who else have I got?*

"I'll do whatever I decide to do, Kane. Take me home."

Kane banged a fist against the steering wheel, then visibly steadied himself, taking two deep breaths before turning to her with a serene smile. "Fine, Grace. Do what you need to do. It's your funeral."

But that was just the problem—maybe it should have been. But it wasn't.

chapter

7

The newspaper staff was at the hospital, reading picture books to sick children.

The cast of the school musical was performing excerpts from *Oklahoma!* at the Grace Retirement Village.

The French club was distributing meals—with a side of croissants, but no wine—to invalids and shut-ins.

Community Service Day was a success, and any senior with a conscience or a guilt complex was devoting the morning to helping others. The only seniors left in class were the ones too lazy to make the effort and too dim to realize that even cleaning bedpans or trimming nose hairs would be preferable to spending the morning in school.

And then there was Beth.

She'd organized the event, worked with the hospital administrators and the town hall community liaison, shined with pride at adding a socially responsible activity to the spirit week agenda, and planned to lead the charge with a quick visit to the Grace animal shelter and a stop at the hospital children's wing, culminating in a triumphant hour of reading to the blind. But instead, she was hiding in an empty classroom, folded over her desk with her head buried in her arms, like she was playing Heads Up, 7 Up all by herself. She'd told her history teacher that she had a headache, but instead of going to the nurse's office, she'd slipped in here and was wiling away her time by listening to her breathing and wondering if Berkeley admitted felons.

She looked up at the sound of a knock on the door. Before she had a chance to come up with a cover story or consider hiding, the door swung open, and Beth was momentarily relieved to realize that it wasn't a teacher who might demand an explanation for Beth's presence. But her relief was short-lived, as a dour-looking woman with a squarish build, coffee-colored skin, and a pinched, vaguely familiar face stepped into the room—followed by a reluctant Harper Grace.

"I was told this room would be empty," the woman said, her words clipped and precise. "You'll have to go."

The woman sat down on one of the desks and, without bothering to check that Beth would follow her command, focused her attention on Harper.

"I should get back to class," Harper mumbled, still standing in the doorway. Beth had to push past her to get out of the room, a maneuver made more difficult by the fact that Harper didn't edge out of the way, but instead just stood planted in the middle of the doorway.

"Come in, sit down," the woman said, and though her voice was soft, it was far from kind. "You said you needed to talk to me—here I am."

Harper glanced toward Beth for the first time, and Beth recoiled from the look in her eyes, a confusing mixture of *Get out* and, more disturbingly, *Stay*. Beth quickened her step. She shut the door behind her, just slowly enough to hear the woman's final words.

"So, what did you remember about the accident?"

She just *had* to come to school today. She couldn't be bothered to tend to the elderly or wipe the brows of the sick—and apparently, this was her punishment. Detective Wells was perched on the edge of one of the desks, while Harper had squeezed herself into a seat, feeling oddly constrained by the metal rod and flat, narrow desk that wrapped around and held her in place. When they called her out of class, she should have known what was coming, but she'd somehow fooled herself into thinking that Wells was a problem that, if ignored, would go away. Not forever, she'd promised herself, screening the latest of the calls, but just long enough that Harper could have a chance to figure out what she was going to do.

Apparently Detective Wells was working on her own timeline.

"I really don't remember what happened," Harper said uncomfortably. The detective's gaze was making her skin crawl, but the alternative views weren't much better. Whoever usually used this classroom had papered the walls with portraits of historical courage—Martin Luther King, Jr., FDR, Rosa Parks, Winston Churchill (she only recognized that one thanks to the oversize caption)—face after face staring down at her with solemn expectation. All she needed was a big painting of Honest Abe to remind her that *some* people "cannot tell a lie." (Or was it George Washington who'd chopped down his cherry tree and then needlessly confessed? Harper could never remember, but she'd always thought that, in the same position, she would have gorged herself on cherries and then enjoyed a sound sleep in the log cabin without giving her sticky red ax a second thought.)

"You left me a message, Harper, saying that you'd remembered *something*." A ridge of wrinkles spread across the detective's forehead. "I don't know why you wouldn't want to help us out, unless—"

"It's just hard," Harper said quickly. *Shut up*, she told FDR's accusing stare. *At least that's true.* "You know, talking about . . . what happened." After struggling for weeks to maintain a mask of contentment, it was tough to make an abrupt shift to visible vulnerability. But Harper didn't know how else to slow things down.

It worked.

"Just take your time," Detective Wells suggested. She leaned forward. "Anything you remember might help us, even if it seems inconsequential."

Harper took a breath and opened her mouth, then shut it again, stalling for time. *You don't know anything,* Kane had said. She wanted to believe him. "I remembered . . . I thought I remembered that the car that hit us was . . . white."

The detective whipped out a notebook and favored Harper with a wide smile. "That's great—anything else?"

"But then, the next night, I had another dream, and the car was black. I guess it was just a dream. Not, you know, a memory," Harper added, wondering if Grace cops got trained in spotting liars. Detective Wells didn't seem much like a human polygraph machine, but you could never tell. "That's why I was, uh, avoiding your calls. I was embarrassed to waste your time."

"It's not a waste," the detective assured her, without bothering to suppress a disappointed sigh. She shut the notebook and stuffed it back into her bag. "You thought you could help, and you did the right thing. No need to be embarrassed about that."

"So . . ." She wasn't sure she actually wanted to know. "Do you have any leads?" Did they even use that word in real life? she wondered. "You know, about what happened? I mean, the other car?"

She shook her head. "We haven't been able to match the paint samples—the van was red, by the way."

"Oh." She wondered why no one had told her that before. She tried to imagine a red van speeding toward her and tried to picture her hands on the wheel, jerking away; but visualization exercises were tough to do when you had to keep your eyes open and smile at a cranky detective.

"We've ascertained that both vehicles were speeding, and that the collision took place on your side of the road, which implies that the driver of the other vehicle may have strayed into your lane, but I'm afraid that's all we know. So far, of course."

"Of course," Harper repeated, although judging from Detective Wells's hopeless and impersonal tone, she guessed that no one really expected to learn much more. "But if you ever did find the guy . . . ?"

"Hit-and-run is a very serious crime," the detective said, looking up at the posters lining the wall. "He or she would be punished to the fullest extent of the law." She scratched the side of her neck, visibly uncomfortable with what she had to say next. "Look, I know it can be difficult, after a traumatic event like this—especially when no one's taken responsibility, and you have no one to blame. There are people you can talk to, if—"

"I'm fine," Harper half shouted. "Can I go back to class now?"

"Sure. Of course. Thanks for speaking with me."

"Sorry you had to come out here for nothing." As Detective Wells shook her hand and headed for the door, Harper could feel her split-second decision hardening into reality. She could still tell the truth—catch the detective before she walked out the door and explain everything—but then the door shut, and the moment had passed.

These are the things I know, Harper told herself.

1. No one knew she was driving, and Kane would never tell.
2. If the van had been in the wrong lane, the accident would have happened anyway, no matter who was driving.
3. Kaia was dead, and she would stay that way, no matter what anyone did.
4. Kaia didn't believe in self-sacrifice.

That left plenty of gaping holes. She didn't know where she'd gotten the drugs from, or why she had taken them. She didn't know why she and Kaia were on the road in the first place, or where they were going. She didn't know whose fault the accident was, not really, though she could pretend that she did. She didn't know if she believed in Hell, so she obviously didn't know if she'd end up there. And she didn't know if she could live with herself—with what she knew and what she didn't—in the meantime.

I have to, she told herself. *And I will.* She looked again at the posters—JFK, Gandhi, Anne Frank, Charles Lindbergh. They must have been from a set made specially for irony-deficient high school teachers, because they all bore some cheesy-beyond-belief quote designed to inspire students.

The nearest way to glory is to strive to be what you wish to be thought to be. Socrates.

He who fears being conquered is sure of defeat. Napoleon.

It's not good enough that we do our best; sometimes we have to do what is required. Winston Churchill.

That one appealed to her the most.

I will do what I have to do and no matter what, I will survive. Harper Grace.

"Where to?"

Beth leaned her head back against the seat and half-heartedly tried to wipe some of the grime off her window, as if the answer to his question might arise from a better view. "Wherever." The word came out as a sigh, fading to silence before the last syllable.

"Okay." Reed drove in circles for a while. He had nowhere to be. When she'd called, he had been at his father's garage, tinkering with an exhaust system and ready for a break. "Can you come?" she'd asked. And for whatever reason, he'd dropped everything and hopped in the truck. He'd found her slouched at the foot of a tree, just in front of the school, hugging her arms to her chest and shivering. She wouldn't tell him anything, but when he extended a hand to help her into the truck, she squeezed.

It's not like they were friends, he told himself. But she

needed something, and he had nothing better to do. He couldn't help but notice that she relaxed into her seat, stretching out along the cracked vinyl, unlike Kaia, who almost always perched on the edge and sat poker-straight in an effort to have as little contact with the "filthy" interior as possible. Beth also hadn't commented on his torn overalls or the smudges of grease splashed across his face and blackening his fingers.

Reed caught himself and, for a moment, felt the urge to stop the car and toss her out on the side of the road. But it passed. "Wanna talk about it?" he asked.

She shook her head. "I don't even want to *think* about it," she said. "Any chance you can take me somewhere where I can do that? Stop thinking?"

She said it bitterly, as if it were an impossible challenge. But she obviously didn't know who she was dealing with.

Reed swung the car around the empty road in a sharp U-turn and pressed down on the gas pedal. She sighed again heavily, and without thinking, he reached over to put a hand on her shoulder, but stopped in midair—maybe because Kaia had trained him well: no greasy fingers on white shirts. Maybe because he didn't want to touch her— or maybe because he did.

He put his hand back on the wheel and began drumming out a light, simple beat. "I know just the place," he assured her. "We'll be there soon." It felt good to have a destination.

Adam crushed the paper into a ball and crammed it into the bottom of his backpack, then butted his head against the wall of a nearby locker—stupid idea, since all it produced was a dull thud and a sharp pain, neither of which went very far toward alleviating his frustration.

But a stupid idea seemed appropriate; after all, what other kind did he have?

Fifty-eight percent.

Maybe if he and Miranda had spent more time working and less time playing video games and talking about Harper . . . At the time, it had seemed like the right thing to do. For those few hours, he'd felt more normal and more hopeful than he had in a long time. Though he and Miranda had never been close, they had history—and, more important, they had Harper. He hadn't needed to confide in her, because she already knew how he felt. And he knew she felt the same.

She was a good friend, he'd realized.

Just maybe not a very good tutor.

Or maybe it's just me, Adam thought in disgust. He'd actually studied this time, staring at the equations long enough that at least a few of them should have started to make sense and weld themselves to his brain. But the test had been a page of incomprehensible hieroglyphics, and Adam's answers—what few he bothered to attempt—were mostly random numbers and symbols that he strung together in an approximation of what he thought an algebra equation should look like.

Thanks to Mr. Fowler's supersonic grading policy—all tests graded and returned by the end of the school day, courtesy of a team of eager beaver honor students who gave up their lunch period for some extra credit and a superiority complex—he didn't have long to wait for the results. Not that there was much suspense.

Fifty-eight percent. It was scrawled in an angry red, next to a big, circled **F** and a note reading *Come see me.*

Instead, Adam dumped his stuff in his locker and walked out of school. It was bad enough he'd had to show up in the first place. Haven teachers were "encouraged" to postpone tests and important lessons for Community Service Day, but Adam's math class was for sophomores and juniors. Which meant enduring both a brain-busting test and the curious stares of his classmates who obviously wondered what kind of loser he was to get left so far behind. Now that he was free for the day, he wasn't going back.

He stomped out of the school, the pounding of his footsteps mirrored by the rhythmic battering of a single word against his brain:

Stupid.

Stupid.

Stupid.

Stupid.

His basketball was in the trunk, and the court across from the school parking lot was empty. It was a no-brainer—fortunately, since his brain was otherwise occupied.

Adam dribbled up and down the court, forcing himself to take it slow and easy. At first the word beat louder, in time with the ball slapping his palm and then slamming into the concrete.

STU-pid.

STU-pid.

STU-pid.

But then he sank his first basket. Adam had always been able to lose himself in the soft sigh of the ball sinking through the net, and today was no different. He emptied his mind and let his body take over, relaxing into the familiar *thwack* and *crack* and *swoosh* that made him feel more alive. Chest heaving, muscles aching, sweat pouring down his face, he didn't notice the time passing or the sky darkening. He stopped only briefly to take a few swigs of water, and again to pull off his shirt and toss it to the sidelines, dimly registering that the scalding afternoon sun had given way to a cool breeze.

He didn't notice Kane step onto the court—it wasn't until the rebound dropped into Kane's hands that Adam looked up. It wasn't the sight of Kane's tall, angular figure poised under the basket that knocked Adam out of the zone; it was the break in the rhythm, when suddenly the expected crack of the ball against pavement was replaced by a soft slap and then silence, as Kane cradled the ball to his chest.

They hadn't faced each other on a basketball court since the game last month, when Adam started a fight with the other team and, in the chaos, flattened Kane, accidentally on purpose. The bruises had taken a couple weeks to fade; Kane's basketball career had dissipated more quickly, as he hadn't returned to practice since.

Kane held the ball and looked at Adam expectantly, his infuriating smirk gone. There were a lot of things Adam could have said—many that he'd said before, many he'd been holding in for a long time:

I thought we were friends.
Did you want Beth, or did you just want to screw with me?
Are you happy now?
We both slept with someone who died.

Are you as freaked out by that as I am?

What happens now?

"Check it," he called, reaching for the ball. Kane bounced it toward him. "First to fifteen."

"Make it twenty-one," Kane suggested, chasing after Adam as he dribbled the ball up the court.

Adam feinted left, then went right, darting around Kane, sprinting toward the basket, and sinking an easy layup. "Done," he agreed.

That was the end of the talking. After that it was all grunting and panting, punctuated by the occasional groan of displeasure as a ball rolled off the rim or a hoot of triumph after a wild shot from the three-point line sailed in with nothing but net. An hour passed, and soon they were playing in the shadows, tracking a sound and a silhouette to chase down the ball, shooting as much by feel as by sight.

Kane sank the final shot. "Twenty-one!" he crowed.

He always won. Adam felt the familiar anger bubble up, but instead of exploding, it just popped and drizzled away, like a string of soap bubbles turning to mist. "Good game," he grunted, slapping Kane's sweaty palm. He grabbed his water bottle and dumped it over his head, closing his eyes and tipping his face up to the cool stream.

"Morgan . . . ?" Kane, who looked as sleek and unruffled as when he'd first appeared, tossed Adam his shirt and a second bottle of water. He rubbed his lower back and looked over toward the empty parking lot. "Look. About . . . everything . . ."

"Forget it, Geary." Adam pulled his shirt on over his dripping torso and grabbed the ball out of Kane's loose grip. He rolled it around in his hands, enjoying the familiar grooves and ridges of its rough grain. "Rematch tomorrow?" he suggested. He turned his back on Kane without waiting for an answer and headed for the car.

"Same time, same place," Kane agreed from behind him, and it was impossible to tell whether his unfailingly sardonic tone masked relief, eagerness, apathy, or regret.

Adam bounced the ball a few times, then tossed it high in the air and caught it with his eyes closed, cupping his hands in a loose cradle and stretching them out to where he knew the ball would be. "I'll be there."

"Aw yeah, that's right." The one named Hale clapped his hands together once as Fish hoisted a giant glass tube out of the crawl space behind the lopsided couch. "Give it here, dude."

"Hold your shit," Fish said, flourishing a lighter.

Beth tucked her hair behind her ears and tried not to look nervous.

Get out, her instincts screamed.

"You okay?" Reed asked, as if he could sense her discomfort. It probably wasn't too hard, she realized, since she was squeezed into the corner of the couch, as far away from Fish as she could get, her arms scrunched up against her sides and her mouth glued shut. She nodded.

"Over here, baby," Hale requested, beckoning Fish to hand over the bong.

"Dude, don't you have any manners?" Fish grabbed one of the discarded fast-food wrappers off the ground, scrunched it up, and threw it at his head. "Ladies first." He stretched across the couch and handed the long, glass tube to Beth, giving her an encouraging nod. She noticed that his hair was even paler than hers, and almost as long.

"Guys, I don't think . . ." Reed, who was perched on an orange milk crate, leaned forward, speaking softly enough that only Beth could hear. "You don't have to. We can go, if you want."

He'd said the same thing when they'd walked into the house and he'd seen the look on her face. There were some empty rooms upstairs, he'd suggested, if she didn't want to hang with the guys—and then he'd flushed, stumbling over his words, hurrying to explain that he hadn't meant *bed*-rooms, not like that. Or they could just go. Anywhere. But for some reason, Beth had insisted they stay, and now here she was, the bong delicately balanced in her hands, nauseating fumes rising toward her, a trippy hip-hop beat shaking the walls—which were covered with fading posters of half-naked women—and for the first time that day, Beth smiled.

"Just tell me what to do," she said firmly. She'd always sworn she wouldn't smoke pot—it was illegal, not to mention dangerous. But she was already a criminal, she reminded herself, and danger didn't scare her anymore—things couldn't get much worse. If she could find a way to turn off her brain, maybe, for a little while, they could actually be better.

Reed didn't try to talk her out of it, and didn't ask about the sudden change of heart. He just rested his hand on top of hers and guided the opening toward her mouth, then gently pressed her finger over a small hole and flicked on the lighter. "Take a deep breath, but don't—"

A spasm of coughing wracked through her body and she inadvertently jerked the bong away, spilling warm, grayish water all over her jeans. "Sorry," she mumbled, her face flushing red.

"No problem. Take a smaller breath the next time," Reed suggested. "And don't uncover the hole until you're ready. Then suck the smoke into your mouth and kind of breathe it down into your lungs."

"Okay, I think—" She broke off as another cough ripped out of her. Reed put his hand on her back, rubbing in small, slow circles.

"Take it easy," he said quietly. "Go slow."

"I'm okay. I'm okay," she protested, straightening up so that he would take his hand away, even though it was the last thing she wanted. "Let me try this again." This time she got a hot lungful down without much coughing. She passed the bong to Fish and leaned back against the couch, waiting for it to take effect.

"Man, this is some good shit!" Fish sputtered as he took his mouth off the tube.

"Totally," Hale agreed after his turn, already looking tuned out to the world.

Reed didn't say anything after his turn, just fixed his eyes on Beth. She looked away, waiting for the room to start spinning or her tongue to start feeling absurdly big. She felt nothing, except the same panic and fear she'd felt for days.

"Time for another little toke," Hale said eagerly, grabbing it back. "Yeah, that's good. Dude, I'm totally high."

"It's like . . . yeah. Cool," Fish agreed.

"Hey, uh . . . Reed's girl, you feeling it?" Hale asked.

Lesson one of getting stoned: Talk about how stoned you are. Beth learned fast. "Yeah," she lied. "It's really wild."

"Dude, Fish, you know what I just realized? You totally look like a girl," Hale cried, a burst of giggles flooding out of him.

Fish ran his fingers through his straggly, straw-colored hair as if realizing it was there for the first time, then looked at Beth in wonderment. "Yeah," he agreed. "And I must be hot. Blondes are *hot.*"

Beth laughed weakly and searched herself for hysteria, paranoia, munchies—*something* to testify to the fact that she'd just ingested an illegal substance for the first time in her life. But she felt, if anything, more self-conscious than ever, as if they could all tell that her mind was running at normal speed and that she was, even here, a total fraud.

"You usually don't feel much the first time," Reed confided, again using that just-for-her voice. "You didn't do it wrong."

Once again, he'd known exactly what she was thinking. A horrifying thought occurred to her: What if he really could tell what she was thinking? What if he knew about Harper, and about Kaia, about everything? And even if he didn't, what would happen if he found out?

Maybe this is paranoia, Beth thought, and now a hysterical giggle did escape her. *Maybe I am high.*

"So, you guys, like, live here?" she asked, trying to make her voice sound as slow and foggy as theirs.

"Fish and Hale do," Reed explained. "And I crash here sometimes."

"He brings his *ladies* here," Hale cackled. "All except—"

"Dude, shut up," Fish snapped, pelting him with another fast-food wrapper—this one seemed to have a chunk of something oozing out of it.

"Oh, yeah. Right. Sorry, bro. Didn't mean to—"

"Whatever." Reed turned the stereo up and then threw himself down on the couch in between Beth and Fish. He leaned his head back, closed his eyes, and kicked his legs up on the milk crate. "Awesome song." He sighed.

When in Rome . . . , Beth thought. *Do as the potheads do.* She closed her eyes, kicked her feet up on the same milk crate so that one leg crossed over Reed's, and forced a serene smile. "I'm, uh, totally hungry," she said tentatively. "Anyone got anything to eat?"

It was such a relief not to have to screen her calls anymore that Harper forgot to play it safe; she forgot that there were still plenty of things she needed to avoid.

"So, I was thinking, tomorrow night," Adam said as soon as she picked up.

"For what?" She lay on her bed, facing away from the window so she wouldn't be tempted to look out for him, or wonder if he was watching her.

"For our date."

"Adam—" she began warningly.

"I paid good money for that date," he pointed out.

"Don't remind me." Her list of humiliating moments was mounting up daily, but stepping onstage for that auction still hovered near the top. "Let's just forget the whole thing."

"Tomorrow night," Adam said again. "Eight. I'll pick you up."

"I told you that I'm not doing this," Harper told him, but she was too tired to fight. "You and me . . ."

"One night. You owe me that."

She sighed. "Fine. Eight. See you then." He started to say something else, but Harper hung up.

It was barely past nine, but she was already in her pajamas. Her homework lay undone—as usual—in a stack on her desk. Her Thoroughly Depressing Music mix (Nick Drake, Norah Jones, Belle and Sebastian, Anna Nalick) was on repeat.

"*'Breathe, just breathe . . . ,'*" she sang along under her breath with the mournful melody. "*'There's a light at each end of this tunnel, you shout 'cause you're just as far in as you'll ever be out . . .'*"

Yeah, right. Everyone had a cliché to offer, and they were all wrong.

Harper was wearing one of Adam's old T-shirts, a Lakers shirt that he'd brought back from his one trip to L.A. a few years ago. Before going, he'd bragged to half the school about going to see Shaq and Kobe play. His mom was dating some real estate hotshot she'd met at a conference, and the guy had gotten them floor seats and all-access passes. He might even get into the locker room, Adam had bragged. But on the night of the game, his mom and her bigwig boyfriend had disappeared for the night, leaving Adam back in the hotel room to watch porn and steal candy from the minibar. He showed up at school the next week wearing the Lakers shirt, full of stories about Shaq's giant feet and the way Kobe had winked at him. Harper was the only one he ever trusted with the truth. She'd borrowed the shirt once last summer, after a drunken water balloon fight had gotten out of hand. She never gave it back.

Summer had been easier, she thought, but then stopped

herself. Even then, things hadn't been right, not really. Adam had been slobbering over Beth while Harper pretended not to care. She imagined she could still see shallow imprints in the heel of each hand from where she'd dug her nails in every time she saw them together, hoping the pain would distract her. She had thought that if she got rid of Beth, somehow, all her problems would just go away. After all, she was Harper Grace—she wasn't supposed to have problems. Ask anyone. She could still remember when that had been true—not last summer, but the one before that, when everything in her life had still made sense.

Kane measures out a small shot of vodka into each of their plastic cups, then tucks the silver flask back into his pocket. Harper puts an arm around Miranda and leans against Adam and, after they clink glasses, downs the shot in a single gulp. A warm tingle spreads through her.

"This idea wasn't nearly as dumb as I thought it was," she admits to Kane, who has dragged them out to the lame ghost town in the dead of night. He gives her a mock bow. They have snuck inside the fake saloon, squeezing up to a table already occupied by plastic mannequins dressed in cowboy clothing. A frozen bartender stands behind the bar, holding a jug of whiskey that will always remain half empty.

"Agreed," Adam says, clapping Kane on the back. "Excellent plan."

"I'm full of them," Kane brags.

Miranda snorts. "Is that why your head's so big?"

He grabs her and puts her in a loose headlock. "Watch it, Stevens," he warns, "or I might be forced to . . ."

"I'm terrified," Miranda says sarcastically. "I'm shaking. What are you going to do?"

Kane doesn't respond, just drives his knuckles into her head and spins. A noogie.

"What are you, ten years old?" Miranda squeals, convulsing in giggles as he lets her go.

Adam and Harper exchange a glance and smile.

"So where's your latest conquest?" Kane asks Adam. "I figured you'd bring her along."

Harper suppresses a laugh. Adam doesn't bring his girlfriends out on excursions like this. They're excess baggage. They'd miss the jokes and spoil the flow of banter honed over the years. They are a foursome, and Adam knows better than to screw with that.

"This one's kind of cute," she tells him, ruffling his hair. "A little bland, but—"

"Who needs a personality when you've got a body like that?" Kane points out, giving them an exaggerated leer. "She's hot."

Miranda smacks him on the shoulder. "She must have some personality—after all, she was too clever to fall for your bullshit."

"I just stepped out of the way and let my man here have a shot," Kane says magnanimously.

Adam, Harper notices, says nothing. It's his turn—now is the time when he chimes in about the annoying way she slurps her soup or the nasal sound of her voice. They always have some minor flaw that becomes insurmountable—too much throat clearing, too many pimples, not enough Simpsons trivia—and then he moves on to the next. It is how things work.

"I'm going to do some exploring," he says instead, standing up.

Harper jumps up. "I'll come along. You guys in?"

Kane puts an arm around one of the mannequins. "What? And leave my friend Buffalo Bob here to drink alone?"

Miranda stays too, and Harper and Adam wander out into the darkness. There are no lights, and she can barely see. She takes

Adam's hand so they don't get separated. It is warm and his grip is strong, and she is not afraid of falling.

"Where do you want to go?" she asks.

He shrugs. "Dunno. I just needed to get out of there."

They wander aimlessly without speaking, past ramshackle buildings whose hokey labels are too difficult to read in the dark. This is the Adam no one else knows, quiet and thoughtful. To everyone else, he is the hot jock, blond and beautiful. To Harper, he is just Adam, who eats his pizza slices crust first, can recite the alphabet backward, and has a tiny scar just behind his left ear. He always capitalizes the word "summer," and flosses his teeth twice every night because he's terrified of getting a cavity. She knows him better than she's ever known anyone.

"So what's the deal?" she asks, shivering as the wind begins to blow. He puts his arm around her and tugs her toward him. She snuggles into his side, where it's warm.

"With what?"

"With the new girl. Beth. Bad breath? Can't stop clearing her throat? Drools when she kisses?"

"Nah, she's good."

"Come on," she says playfully. "It's always something. You can tell me."

"It's weird, Gracie." His voice isn't playful at all. "It's not like that. She's . . . different."

"Oh, I get it." Harper squeezes her arm around his waist. "You're still in that nauseating 'everything is wonderful' stage. Ah, young lust. So romantic."

"No." He stops walking and drops his arm away from her shoulder. "It really is different this time. It's . . . she's . . ." He holds his hands out to his sides. She can't see his face in the dark. "I can't explain. There's just something about her."

"I understand, Ad." And she does. She throws her arms around him and hugs him tightly. "I'm really happy for you." And she wants to mean it. She knows she should mean it, but as she holds him, her face burrowed into his shoulder, breathing in the familiar mix of fabric softener and a woodsy aftershave, she realizes something important. And then she squeezes tighter. She doesn't want to let go, because when she does, everything will change.

Harper turned out the light and curled up into a ball, trying to sleep. Her leg throbbed and her back ached, and the T-shirt felt uncomfortably tight around her collar. It kept getting caught beneath her weight as she rolled to one side, then the other. It was tugging at her and choking her, keeping her from sinking into sleep. Eventually she wriggled out of it and tossed it to the floor. It didn't even smell like him anymore.

chapter

8

"Tell me you're free tonight."

"Uh . . . what? Who is this?" But Miranda knew who it was. She would have recognized the voice even if she hadn't recognized the number (which she'd memorized back in ninth grade).

"I'm bored," Kane said, affecting a little kid voice. "Come play with me?"

Her chest tightened, and a warm glow spread through her cheeks. *Not a date,* she reminded herself. But the caution had little effect. He wanted to see her; that had to mean something.

"It's kind of short notice," she pointed out, toying with him. "A true lady wouldn't accept an offer made in such haste."

"Well then, it's a good thing you're not—"

"Don't even say it," she warned. This whole banter thing was so much easier when he wasn't there to see the crimson flush rising in her cheeks. She could put her hand over the mouthpiece whenever she needed to mask her giggles and gasps. It was easy to sound cool and unconcerned.

He laughed—a rich, warm sound made all the sexier by the knowledge that she'd caused it.

"There's this thing, kind of a pre-party, and it'll probably be lame, but I thought I'd check it out," he explained.

"Pre-party? So I'm not good enough to take to the *actual* party?" She sounded sarcastic, but couldn't help but fear it was true.

"Insecurity doesn't suit you, my dear. The actual party's tomorrow night—this is just a little warm-up."

"Why not?" She tried not to sound too eager.

"Cool. You think you can give me a ride? I figure, in case I get wasted . . ."

Well, that solved the mystery. He just needed a designated driver; it's not that he thought he'd have fun with her, it's that he knew she could be trusted *not* to have any fun. She pressed her palm against the mouthpiece and sighed. It didn't matter why he had called. She would go, anyway, just as she would spend the next half hour tormenting herself about what to wear, even though she'd already convinced herself that he didn't want anything from her beyond the occasional ride and no-strings-attached hookup. There was always a chance, and even an eternal pessimist like Miranda couldn't help but cling to that.

Adam brought her to The Whole Enchilada, her favorite restaurant—as Kaia had often pointed out, there was no *good* food in Grace, but the local Mexican food came the closest. Harper hadn't wanted to admit that she was addicted to their guacamole ("could be fresher," according to Kaia) and loved their burritos ("overstuffed"), but both girls agreed that the stale chips and crappy salsa—half as spicy and twice as watery as you'd want—were worth suffering through for the oversize frozen margaritas. They were frothy and sweet, with a double shot of tequila—and served by waiters who could be counted on not to card.

Tonight, Harper sipped a Coke.

She hadn't said much after hello, nor had she bothered to listen as Adam babbled on about his latest basketball game or some lame joke the guys had pulled on their coach. She'd ordered a chicken enchilada, but when it appeared in front of her, she couldn't even imagine eating it. She nibbled at the edges, crunched down on a couple chips, and drank a lot of water. It was a waste of a meal, but then, Adam was paying—so who cared?

"You know, my grandfather died when I was a kid," he said abruptly.

She froze, a forkful of rice halfway to her mouth. She'd been expecting him to bring up Kaia, and she'd readied herself to shoot him down. But she didn't have a contingency plan for this.

"He was the only grandparent I had," Adam continued. "My dad's parents, they kind of . . . disappeared, or something. Before I was born. And my mom's mom died when she was a kid. But my grandfather was around for a while, and when he died, you know, it was really sudden. It sucked."

Harper felt like she was supposed to say something. "Yeah."

"I didn't, uh, I didn't really get it, at first. I was just a kid. I kept asking my mom why we didn't go over to see him anymore, and then she'd just start freaking out and crying. So then after a while, I just stopped asking." He gave her a weird look, half determined and half scared. Harper wondered what he expected now: Did he think that just mentioning someone dying was going to make her cry, and then he'd have to mop up the mess? "I know it's not the same, or anything . . ."

"No," she agreed.

"The worst part was that I was all alone with it, you know? So I just thought, maybe . . ."

She gave him a faint "Where are you going with this?" smile. She wasn't going to make it easier on him.

Adam squirmed in his seat. Touchy-feely stuff wasn't really his style. "You can talk to me. About how you're feeling. About . . . anything."

He wanted to know how she was feeling.

She felt numb.

She felt hollow, like a black hole at her center had sucked away her insides, only no one could tell because the outer shell was still intact.

She felt angry all the time, at Adam, at her parents, at the world, at herself. And she didn't know why.

Her thoughts were jumpy and sluggish at the same time, skipping from subject to subject only because by the time she got to the middle of a thought, she forgot where she'd started or where she was going. So she felt lost.

She felt like crying every time she laughed, and she rarely felt much like laughing.

She felt heavy.

She felt unworthy.

She felt like if someone touched her in the right way, she might disintegrate.

She could turn off the tears and paint on a smile whenever she needed to, which made her wonder if the tears weren't real either. She felt like a fraud.

But she wasn't about to tell him any of that.

"I feel fine," she said coolly. She pushed her plate toward his side of the table. "Want to try some? I'm done."

"BETH!"

"We're BOOOOOOOOOOORED!"

"I'll be down in a minute!" she yelled, gulping down a couple Advil tablets. It was nice that her parents got to spend a romantic evening out on the town while she took care of the twins, she knew—and it wasn't like she could have turned them down, given the fact that she had no other plans—but handling the twins' hyperactive sugar craze was about the last thing she needed right now.

She picked up the envelope and pulled out the letter, even though she didn't need to read it again. It was short, and she'd already memorized it.

No one got mail these days, so although it was probably still too early for college acceptances to arrive, she'd let herself get excited, anyway, just for a moment, when her mother had returned from the mailbox and tossed a letter toward her.

Her first reaction: It was thin. She was screwed.

But then she took a closer look and realized it wasn't from a college at all. Her name and address were handwritten, as was the return address, a P.O. Box in Texas. She didn't know anyone in Texas.

She was mystified, but some part of her—maybe the

153

part that was always watching and worrying these days, waiting for something awful to happen—made her take the letter upstairs so she could open it in private. Her father was at the kitchen table pouring over bills, and her mother had already turned her attention toward the high-maintenance part of the family. When Beth slipped up to her room, no one even noticed.

She'd been up there ever since, coming out only briefly to say good-bye to her parents and receive the standard lecture about emergency contact numbers and keeping the boys away from sugar, fire, and electrical sockets. She'd nodded and pretended to listen, like playing the responsible and dutiful daughter hadn't become more of an act than a reality, and then gone back to her room, figuring the twins could fend for themselves, at least until it was time to heat up some leftover pizza and watch *SpongeBob*.

The letter, more of a note, really, scrawled on a slip of hotel stationery, had come stapled to a familiar clipping from the *Grace Herald*.

Student-Teacher Scandal Rocks Haven High

Two phrases were highlighted in light green:

"We're all grateful that they had the courage [to turn Payne in] and prevent this from happening again,"

and

district officials say they had no sign Powell was not what he seemed

The attached note was only a few lines long: *Good to know I can always count on you . . . to keep your mouth shut. See you soon? JP.*

"Beth!" There was a loud pounding at the door. "Come play with us," Jeff begged—although their voices were as identical as their faces, she was sure it was him. He always took the lead.

"Yeah, or we'll tell Mom!" And that would be Sam, who could always be counted on to tattle.

Beth folded the letter and the clipping and stuffed them back in the envelope, which she stuck in her top desk drawer, beneath a box of paper clips and old stationery. She shouldn't throw it out—what she should do, in fact, was take it to the police and explain everything. But she knew she wouldn't. What if no one believed her story? Or worse, what if everyone did? The way they would all look at her, unable to believe that good, reliable Beth had gotten herself involved in something so publicly tawdry. . . .

And that was just the best-case scenario.

What if Powell came back to town? What if he realized she *wouldn't* keep her mouth shut, and decided to shut it for her?

Or what if the police decided to check into her story and started digging into her life? If anyone started asking questions, if anyone found out about the box of pills, about what she had done—no. She couldn't risk it. She would hold on to the letter, on the off chance that she found some secret store of courage somewhere within her.

But she wasn't holding her breath.

"Okay," she said wearily, opening the door. Jeff and

Sam launched themselves at her, each grabbing hold of one of her legs. "What do you two brats want to do?"

"I'm not a brat," Jeff complained, turning his head up and sticking out his lower lip.

"I am!" Sam shouted, and poked Jeff in the shoulder. "See? Brat! Brat! Brat! Brat!" Each time he yelled the word, he poked Jeff again. Jeff scrunched up his face, squinted, turned bright red, and then began to scream.

"Aaaaaaagh!" he shouted, hurling himself toward Sam with his fingers extended like claws. "I'll get you!" But Sam, sensing that his brother was about to blow, had already taken off down the hall.

Beth sagged against the wall as the two chased each other through the house, hooting and growling. She gave herself two minutes, silently counting off the seconds in her head until she could justify it no longer, and then ran down the hallway, hoping to find a way to tame the wild beasts.

An hour later, she'd gotten them tucked into a blanket on the couch, one on either side of her, both staring blissfully at SpongeBob and friends. It occurred to her that her parents had wanted her to do something constructive with them—the twins each had a thick workbook with "fun" activities about telling time and counting money. But that would require thinking, and none of the Manning children was up to that tonight. It was so much easier just to snuggle on the couch and relax in the flickering light of the TV. Beth tugged the blanket toward her neck and closed her eyes, trying to forget. . . .

"Beth! Wake up!" Jeff shouted, shaking her shoulder. "You're missing the best part."

Her eyes popped open, just in time to see a dark figure creep across the screen, lurching toward a peacefully sleeping child. She must have fallen asleep, and the twins must have taken the opportunity to change the channel, unless this was a Very Special Episode, "SpongeBob Goes on a Killing Spree."

Sam and Jeff burrowed into her sides, pressing her hands over their eyes but peeking out just enough to see what was happening. Beth knew she should change the channel, but she couldn't find the remote, and she didn't really want to get up. . . .

The figure came closer to the sleeping boy, and the eerie music rose in the background.

Closer and closer, until—

"Aaaah!" the boys screamed in unison as a knife slashed down. Beth leaped off the couch and switched off the TV.

"Just a movie," she said cheerfully.

But it was too late. That night, it was impossible to get them to sleep. They wouldn't let her turn out the light, and kept asking if "He" was going to come and get them. Feeling guilty—as if she ever felt any other way, these days—Beth let them sleep in her bed, together, and promised to sit by their sides until they fell asleep.

Eventually, Sam closed his eyes and fell silent, but Jeff couldn't stop whimpering.

"Shhh," Beth said, putting a hand against his forehead. They always looked so small and sweet in their pajamas, tucked under the covers, impossibly innocent about the way anything worked. As if it were the bogeyman they really needed to be afraid of.

"I'm scared," Jeff whispered.

"There's nothing to be scared of," Beth assured him. "I'll protect you."

"Aren't you scared?" he asked, wide-eyed.

"No." She leaned down and kissed his forehead, then kissed Sam, too, gently so that he wouldn't wake up. "I told you, there's nothing to be scared of."

No wonder he couldn't fall asleep; lamer words were never spoken.

Miranda wasn't sure whether the house was abandoned or just a pigsty; it was hard to tell in the candlelight. About thirty people, mostly drunk or high, were scattered around the grounds—smoking in the backyard, making out in the bedrooms, experimenting with mixers in the kitchen. Miranda and Kane were sprawled out on a dusty couch in the living room. They'd snagged the best spot; most of the other couples were stuck lounging on the floor or leaning against each other in secluded corners. It wasn't much like any party Miranda had ever been to; there was very little "partying" going on, as far as she could tell. There wasn't even any music.

Not that she cared, not while Kane leaned against her, one hand cradling a beer and the other idly playing with her hair. Was he desperately wishing he could take her off somewhere private and have his way with her? Was he struggling with his fear of intimacy, wondering if his newly discovered love for her could overpower his nerves, and if he could convince her that he was serious about making things work?

Miranda doubted it, but it was a fun fantasy (courtesy, in part, of an afternoon with *Dr. Phil*). She could lean over and kiss him right now. But she wanted more than that, she reminded herself. She wasn't that kind of girl. Her friendship didn't come with benefits.

"Sorry this sucks," Kane said, his voice slow and heavy the way it got when he was a little drunk. Miranda almost liked him better this way; the cold, sneering veneer fell away and, every once in a while, he was actually nice. She'd always told herself this was the real Kane—alcohol just let him come out and play. "I should have known better."

"It's fine," she assured him. "I'm having fun."

He snorted, almost spitting out his mouthful of beer. "Yeah, right. Tell me something," he said, stretching out along the couch and lying down, his head in her lap. He looked up at her. "This okay?" She nodded, not trusting herself to speak. His hair fell back from his forehead, splaying out across her leg. It was so unbelievably smooth.

"Tell you what?" she asked, resisting the urge to stroke his forehead.

"I don't know," he said, slurring his words slightly. "Why you're so sad."

"I'm not sad," she protested.

He nodded as well as he could with his head resting on her legs. "Are too. Sad Miranda."

"I'm not sad right now," she pointed out, leaning over him so he could see her grin.

He reached up and touched her lips. "Can't fool me."

She didn't know how drunk he was; maybe he wouldn't even remember this in the morning, which would be better. All she knew was that she *was* sad—and it had been a long time since anyone had noticed, or wanted to know why.

"It's Harper," she admitted, feeling a hint of relief now

that she'd finally said it out loud, even to Kane, who would probably make a joke out of it as he did about everything else. "Everything I say is wrong, and she doesn't want to talk to me, and it's like we're not even friends anymore." The words came fast and furiously; she'd been afraid that if she said it out loud, she would make it real. But saying it out loud was better than saying it to herself, over and over again.

"She's just . . . upset."

"*I'm* upset!" Miranda exclaimed. She stopped herself and took a deep breath. It felt almost like she was talking to herself. "I want to be a good friend to her, but . . . I also, I just . . ." She put her hands over her face, humiliated to realize it was wet with tears. "I miss having a best friend," she choked out.

"Hey," he said in alarm, pushing himself up. His breath was sour and his eyes glassy, but she didn't care. "Hey, don't—" He wrapped his arms around her and she clung to him, for once not wondering what he was thinking or wishing she could kiss him. She just closed her eyes and tried to catch her breath. "She'll be back," he promised, and much as she wanted to believe him, she knew he was just saying it. Guys would say anything to get a girl to stop crying.

"I hate being alone," she mumbled into his soggy collar.

He pushed her away, just far enough that he could see her face, and he held her in place so she couldn't look away. "Stevens, you're not," he said firmly.

"I know," she said, nibbling at the edge of her lip. "It's just . . ."

"No. You're *not.*"

She wanted him so much, suddenly, that she couldn't

breathe. His lips were half parted, and his eyes, usually so cold, now seemed like warm, inviting pools of deep brown. She bit down on the inside of her cheek, hoping the pain would make her ignore how good, how *safe* it felt to have his arms around her.

Maybe this was right after all; maybe it didn't matter that he was drunk and horny and she was in love—maybe they could meet in the middle, just for tonight.

"I have to go," she said, forcing the words out.

"What?"

"Just for a minute. I just need . . . I need some air. I have to go outside," she said, trying to convince herself as much as anything.

"Do you want me to . . . ?"

"Stay." She put a hand on his bicep and suppressed a shudder. "I'll be right back. And . . . Kane?"

"Yeah, Stevens?"

"Thanks."

Things weren't going as well as he'd expected, although now that dinner was done—Harper's meal nearly untouched, Adam's plate scraped clean—and the bill paid, Adam had to admit that he didn't know what he'd expected. His auction bid had been a spur-of-the-moment thing, but over the last few days he'd built it up in his head into his big last chance. It seemed that, despite his carefully chosen clothes—the light green button-down shirt that she loved and he hated, khakis that usually only left his closet when his mother forced him to go to church—this day was going to end the same as all the rest. Unless he did something.

"I thought we'd walk home," he suggested, hoping to delay the inevitable.

Already halfway to his car, she turned and gave him a weird look. "You didn't even have anything to drink. And, FYI, your car's right here."

"It's such a nice night," he pointed out, fully aware that it was a kind of girly thing to say.

Harper shrugged. "Yeah. Whatever." Translation: *You forced me into this, and I'm just counting the minutes until the night is over.*

They walked along the side of the road in silence. The sidewalks were deserted; most of Grace's nightlife was limited to the dive bars and greasy taverns lining the side streets, and their patrons wouldn't be stumbling out for hours. Main Street—home of assorted failing small businesses and several gas stations—was shuttered and dark. They could have been alone in the world.

Harper shivered, and Adam wondered if she'd had the same thought, or if she was just cold. He didn't ask, nor did he offer his jacket, knowing she'd turn it down.

It took him about ten minutes to work up his courage, then another five to figure out how to express what he needed to say—but when that proved to be a doomed effort, he just started talking. "I miss you, Gracie," he told her.

She didn't even look at him. He stopped walking and grabbed her arm, forcing her to stop too. They stood in the shadows of Shopsin's Shoes, which had closed months before and was now boarded up and empty. Harper tapped her foot and looked over his shoulder.

"I miss you," he said again.

"I'm right here."

"No you're not," he argued.

She crossed her arms and scowled, looking like a pouty child. "Can we *go* now?"

"I want you back."

She rolled her eyes. "As a friend. Yeah. I know."

"What's wrong with that?"

"What's wrong with something more than that?" she challenged him.

"Harper, you know—" He stopped himself. He didn't know how to put it into words, that feeling he got when he felt her getting too close, some strange mix of anger, fear, repulsion—and desire. It was all too much. "We already talked about this," he said vaguely.

"I want to hear you say it," she sneered. "I want to hear you say exactly what you think of me. Exactly what kind of person you think I am."

"I don't . . . I don't know what you want from me."

She took a step toward him, then another. And then suddenly, she was on top of him, her arms threaded through his and her fingers digging into the skin of his lower back, then scraping up his back toward his neck. "I want *this*," she hissed. She lifted her right leg, rubbing her thigh against him, and she sucked in his lips, nibbling, biting the edges and shoving her tongue into his mouth as her hands began tearing at his hair, squeezing his face and pressing it into hers. There was friction, heat, rubbing, pulling, kneading, sucking, moaning—and then silence as he pushed her away.

"What the hell are you doing?" he asked, his face hot and his breathing rapid. There was something so ugly about her naked need, and it pained him to realize that an angry, primal part of him wanted to grab her back and finish what she'd started.

"You think I'm a slut," she spit out. Her eyes were wide and her face was unnaturally pale, while her voice was nearly an octave higher than usual, which sometimes happened when she got too angry.

"I don't—"

"You *do*. A shallow slut that you can be *just friends* with"—her face contorted in pain at the words—"but why would a slut want to be friends with a guy like you if she can't get something out of it?" She stepped toward him again, and before he could back away, she shoved him in the chest, hard. "All I want is sex, right? *Right?*" Another shove. "And if you can't give it to me, what the hell good are you? Why wouldn't I just go find it somewhere else?"

Maybe that's where she was headed when she stalked away. Adam didn't know, and he didn't follow.

Miranda took a deep breath and stepped back into the house, ready to rejoin the party—or at least rejoin Kane. But her seat was taken. Kane lay in the same position as before, his head now in the lap of a curvy junior cheerleader who was running her fingers lightly up and down his face.

She didn't want to get any closer. But she didn't have much other option, unless she wanted to start up a conversation with the couple making out to her right, or the guy passed out on her left. Kane had a short attention span; maybe he'd just gotten bored while she—perhaps rudely—left him alone. It was possible the girl was just a diversion and he'd get rid of her as soon as he saw Miranda.

But he didn't see Miranda. It would have been pretty much impossible for him, what with the 110-pound cheerleader now attached to his lips. Feeling sickened, Miranda sank back on one of the arms of the couch, trying to look away but compelled to keep glancing at them. Kane wasn't doing much, just lying there, as the girl rubbed his face and started kissing down his neck.

"Hey," he said suddenly, spotting Miranda now that his face was clear. The cheerleader didn't even look up—she was too busy nuzzling his chest. Kane gave Miranda a lazy grin. "Party's not so bad after all."

Miranda couldn't force her mouth into a smile, so she settled for a thin, wobbly line.

"So, are you—" But Kane broke off into a spasm of laughter as the cheerleader began tickling his sides. "I don't *think* so," he mock growled, and flipped her over on the couch so that he was on top, perfectly positioned for some tickling torture of his own.

It was like Miranda wasn't there anymore.

She tried not to cry.

The room was dark, and nearly silent, but she felt like everyone was staring at her, wondering what that loser was doing. Maybe she looked like some kind of pervert, spying on Kane as he made out with his latest floozy. It's not like she wanted to keep standing there. But she didn't have anywhere else to go.

The minutes dragged by.

And as she stood there, her back unnaturally straight and her hands clenched into fists, her tears dried up. *Screw him,* she thought. Bringing her here, acting like he cared, then ditching her as soon as she left the room. Let him find his own ride home.

"I'm out of here," she said softly, as if experimenting with the words. There was no response from the couple on the couch.

"Kane, I'm out of here," she said, louder this time.

He flicked his gaze up toward her. "Cool. I can get a ride home from . . ."

"Kelli," the junior giggled into his ear. "With an 'i.'"

Of course. It was always with an i.

"Fine," she snapped. He didn't need her; she didn't need him. Whatever. *Screw him. Screw him. Screw him.* "Screw you!" It popped out before she realized she was going to say it, and it felt good. She stood up and strode out of the "party," stepping over two guys passed out on the floor and narrowly avoiding a collision with some jock who was lurching toward the door, his face a disconcerting shade of green.

The car was parked about half a block away, and she walked quickly, her thoughts keeping time with her footsteps. *I don't need him. I don't want him. I don't need him. I don't want him.*

"Hey, Stevens, what gives?"

She whirled around at the touch of his hand on her shoulder and shrugged him off. "Where's your *friend*?" she sneered.

"Are you mad?" His eyes were wide and innocent, but it was hard to tell whether he was playing oblivious for effect or whether the alcohol really had numbed his brain enough to make it true.

She was totally sober, but apparently her judgment control had forgotten that. "Why would I be mad?" she yelled. "You drag me to this *pit* and then you ditch me for some . . . You're such an asshole!"

"Uh . . ." He looked dazed, as if she'd hit him in the head. Then a slow grin spread across his face. "Jealous, Stevens? Did you think that we . . ."

She told herself not to blush, but she could feel the heat rise in her cheeks. "No! No."

"Then what?"

Her righteous anger faded away, because, of course, she *was* jealous. She was also certain that she had every right to be mad, jealous or not—but she couldn't quite figure out why, not with Kane standing so close and the corners of his eyes crinkling up so hotly. "It was just rude," she complained, hating herself for not being able to hate him. She turned away and kept walking toward her car, ignoring the footsteps that followed behind her.

"What are you doing?" she asked finally as she opened the car door and he stood by the passenger's side, waiting for it to be unlocked.

"What's it look like?"

"Go back to the party," she said, suddenly too tired to fight, with him or with herself.

"I'm going home with you," he said stubbornly. "You're still mad."

"Kane, I'm not mad." She sighed. "Just go back to the party. You're allowed to do whatever you want."

"I want to go home with you," he said. "I didn't mean that the way it sounded . . . unless . . ."

"Forget it, buddy."

"Let's go," he said, getting into the car and snapping on his seat belt.

Miranda shook her head. "I think I can handle the ten-minute drive on my own. Go back to the party."

"Stevens, when are you going to learn? I *am* the party." He leaned across the bucket seats and laid a hand on her thigh. "If you want, we can have a little party of our own. . . ."

She took his hand away, but before she could drop it back to his side, he squeezed and they paused like that, their hands joined in midair. All she could hear was their breathing, hers rapid and fluttery, his labored and heavy. She pressed her lips together and dropped his hand. "Okay, party boy, let's get you home."

She started the ignition, and he flicked a lock of her hair over her shoulder, forcing her to turn toward him again and face his crooked, knowing smirk. "Have it your way, Stevens. But you don't know what you're missing."

Let's see, she thought wryly, *that would be: pain, lust, heartbreak, torture.*

Although, come to think of it, her personal inventory already had plenty of those items in stock. So she wasn't missing a thing.

It didn't seem real and it didn't make sense, but it was happening. Harper pressed herself against the wall. She wanted to look away—she wanted to run away—but her feet were stuck to the floor. She couldn't move, and when she tried to speak, nothing came out.

There was no light in the room, but somehow, she could see everything clearly.

Adam on his back, in his boxers. Kaia straddling him, her

head tossed back, her black hair splashed out behind her.

Stop! Harper shouted, and even though her lips didn't move, she could hear the word echoing through the room. Kaia and Adam didn't notice.

"Are you ready?" Kaia whispered. She kissed his chin. She kissed his neck. She licked his nipples, one by one. Adam moaned.

So did Harper.

"I've been waiting for you," Adam said, unlatching her lacy black bra and letting it drop to the floor.

Kaia made a noise that sounded like a purr. "I know." She slipped her fingers under Adam's head and jerked it toward hers, giving him a long, sloppy kiss. Then she turned and looked directly at Harper. "He doesn't want you," she sneered, giving Harper a cruel smile. "He wants me. They all do."

Shut up! Harper screamed silently. It felt like her throat was choked with cotton. She tried to close her eyes, but they wouldn't shut.

Kaia shimmied down Adam's body until she reached the waistband of his boxers. She slipped her thumb between his skin and the cotton and began, ever so slowly, to pull them off.

"I hate you!" Harper shrieked, finding her voice. The words exploded from her lungs and filled the room, which seemed to shake with the noise. Adam half sat up and looked across the room at Harper, shaking his head sadly. Kaia touched his chin to stop the motion, then kissed him again. *"I hate you!"* Harper shouted again, feeling the power of her wrath course through her body.

And then she woke up.

Drenched, shivering beneath her covers, tears streaking her face.

Harper turned over on her stomach, burrowing her face into the pillow. "I'm sorry!" she gasped, fighting for breath. "I'm sorry. I'm sorry. I'm sorry. I'm sorry." She murmured the words over and over again until her breathing slowed and she stopped shaking. But that night, she didn't fall back asleep.

chapter

9

There were no invitations. Word traveled, and everyone just knew where to show up, and when. Senior Spirit Week was for the teachers and the administration so they could feel good about offering their students some good, clean fun. But everyone knew that senior spring only officially began at midnight, in the midst of debauchery and revels. There was a spot out in the desert, a shallow wash of scrub-brush surrounded by clumps of Joshua trees on one side and a stretch of low, rocky ridges on the other. It was tradition. The cops allowed it. The administration ignored it. Parents pretended it didn't exist—although most of them had been through it themselves, twenty years before. It signified the beginning of the end, a night of wild release that, if all went well, would be whispered about for years. Graduation was a hot, tedious hassle; prom was a chance for girls to spend too much on evening dresses and guys to get that last precollege shot at losing their virginity. *This* was a rite of passage.

Beth had decided not to go.

Then she changed her mind.

After an hour of flip-flopping, she was standing in front of her mirror wearing standard-issue black pants, a shimmery blue, scoop-neck top that matched her eyes, and a sparkly bracelet she'd gotten for her birthday last year but never taken out of the box. She swept her hair up into a high, lose ponytail, wishing the long, blond strands would wave or curl or do anything other than fall limply down to her shoulders. She dabbed on some glittery gray eye shadow and a layer of clear gloss.

And she still wasn't sure she was going to leave the house.

Her original plan had been to never leave the house *again*, but that seemed less than feasible.

She'd come up with a variety of rationales:

If she didn't start acting normal, people would suspect something was going on, and she couldn't afford that.

She would likely have a terrible time, so she didn't need to feel guilty.

If she wasn't going to turn herself in—because, she reminded herself, she hadn't intentionally hurt anyone, and not because she was a pathetic coward—she had to start living her life again at some point.

None of them were nearly as persuasive as the deciding factor: Reed's band was playing the party. And, much as she hated to admit it, she wanted to see him again.

There was nothing going on, she assured herself. She and Reed were a nonissue—even if it hadn't been for . . . what had happened with Kaia. Reed was the opposite of her type, and last time she'd played that game, she'd lost big.

If she was going to get involved with anyone again, it would be someone sweet and quiet, who was kind to children and animals and cared about getting into college, going to class, and doing the right thing.

Except: Why would someone like that ever want to be involved with her? She wasn't Beth Manning, golden girl, anymore. She'd stopped going to class, probably wouldn't get into college—and had proven once and for all that, unless it was painless, she wouldn't do the right thing.

If she was being honest with herself, she knew she couldn't get involved with anybody. Lonely as she was, she couldn't afford something open, honest, or *real*. She couldn't invite someone into her life and trust him with her secrets and her fears.

Still, she slipped on a jacket and wrapped a pink scarf around her neck, waved good-bye to her parents, and walked out the door. She'd never heard Reed play before, and she was just curious, she assured herself. Miserable, bored, scared, and curious. That's all there was to it.

Miranda drained her plastic cup and stuck it under the keg, pumping until a frothy flow spurted out. It tasted like shit, but she forced it down, anyway. The world tipped a bit to the left, then righted itself before she could fall over, but she still felt like things would start spinning if she turned her head too fast.

Perfect.

There he was, less than ten feet away, standing at the fringes of a group of jocks trying to set fire to a cactus. He looked disgusted—and hot. Miranda stumbled toward him, sneaking up behind him and slapping her hands over his eyes.

"Geary," she whispered, holding back a giggle. "Guess who?"

He spun around, and she hopped up and gave him an impulsive kiss on the cheek. "I'm drunk," she announced giddily.

He looked her up and down, then patted her on the head. "Thanks, Captain Obvious. I got that."

She felt so free. "You like?" she asked, twirling around to show off her outfit, a dark green corset and very un-Miranda-like skin-tight pants.

"Nice." He ran his hand down the laced up sides of her shirt. "*Very* nice."

Before the party, she'd decided: It doesn't count if you're drunk. Everyone knew this party was about doing things you shouldn't—and so why should she deny herself the one thing she knew she absolutely, under no circumstances, if she wanted to keep her sanity or her dignity, shouldn't do? She just needed to work up a little safety buzz—get just drunk enough to serve as an excuse for anything that might happen. Anything she hoped would happen. She'd thought it all out, and it had made perfect sense.

Four beers later, she was done thinking. "You look good," she said, stepping toward him and nearly falling as the ground shifted beneath her feet. Or, at least, it seemed to. "Whoops," she squeaked as he caught her in his big, strong, muscular, tan arms. "Did I mention I'm a *little* drunk?"

"Did I mention this is a new shirt?" Kane asked wryly. "Don't puke on it."

He slung an arm around her waist and walked her away from the crowd, sitting her down on the ground so she wouldn't have too far to fall.

"Hey!" she called, tugging on the leg of his jeans. "It's lonely down here."

Kane crouched down next to her.

"Hi!" she said in her best sultry voice, leaning toward him.

He flinched away from her breath. "Jesus—did you drink the whole keg?"

This wasn't going right. Miranda struggled to figure out where she'd run off track, but her brain was like a see-saw, swinging wildly back and forth, up and down . . . and at the thought of that, she felt a wave of nausea rise in her. So she stopped thinking again and just blurted something out. "This isn't going right."

Oops.

"What isn't?"

Instead of answering, Miranda leaned against him and let her head drop to her shoulder. "The music's nice, huh?"

Kane glanced over at the Blind Monkeys, who were banging something out that approximated a song. "You call this music?"

"I love your smile," Miranda slurred, touching his lips. "It's so . . . smiley."

He frowned, took her hand, and peered into her eyes. "You in there somewhere, Stevens? 'Cause I think some kind of pod person's taken over your body."

He was so funny. "You're so funny." She laughed, her body twitching uncontrollably, until finally she pressed both her hands against her mouth to stop herself. "D'you want to kiss me?" she asked suddenly, taking her hands away and pursing her lips.

"Uh, Stevens . . ."

"'Cause you can. I'm right here." She let herself fall

toward him, but at the last moment, he grabbed her shoulders and held her at arm's length.

"I'm not sure we should—"

"Hey!" she cried, suddenly distracted. "It's Harper!" She started waving wildly. "Harper!" But Harper was too far away. "She's mick of see. I mean. She's sick of me. I mean. You know. What I mean." Some sleazy guy in cargo shorts with a studded collar around his neck was leading Harper away from the band and toward the more private, shadowy area beyond the rocks.

"You know that guy?" Kane asked suspiciously.

Miranda shook her head. The sleazeball swooped in for a kiss and Harper pulled herself away—but she wasn't quick enough. They made out for a minute, and then the guy continued leading her away.

"She's even drunker than me." Miranda giggled, then stopped as a pinhole of light opened up in the dark fog of her mind. "What's she doing with that guy? What if—?" Her happy buzz turned into an angry beehive. "We have to stop her," she said, trying to stand up. She shook her head, but that just made things more jumbled. "We have to go, we have to—"

"Whoa. Better idea." Kane pressed down firmly on her shoulders, settling her back on the ground. "I'll go. You stay."

"But I have to help, I have to—"

"I'm sure it's fine," he assured her. "I'll go. I'll take care of it. Are you okay here?"

"My knight in shining armor." She sighed, a happy glow settling over her again. Kane would take care of everything, and then he'd be back for her.

"Yeah, that's me," he scoffed. "Just try not to wander off and get into trouble before I get back, princess."

As he disappeared into the crowd in search of Harper, Miranda sighed happily and lay back against the ground, staring up at the stars and wondering if she could find the Big Dipper.

He'd be back soon—and she wasn't going anywhere.

Forgive, forget; the wavy lines on my TV
Go dark as you, betray your confidences on—

Reed broke off in disgust. The sound system was crap, and he could barely hear himself sing over the drunken crowd—not to mention the fact that he was pretty sure someone was blasting Beyoncé on a stereo not too far away. But that wasn't the real issue.

"Fish!" he snapped, spinning around to look at the drummer. "What the hell are you doing back there?"

"Man, I forgot what song we were playing." He giggled. "Can you believe that?"

"Dude, you're totally baked!" Hale mocked, waving his guitar over his head. "Awesome."

Reed knocked the microphone away in disgust. "You're both playing for shit. Get it together."

"Take it easy, kid," Fish suggested. "I can fire up another one for you."

"Let's just play," Reed said, half tempted, half disgusted. "'Miles from Home,' okay? On three?" They nodded, and Fish counted off; Hale came into the song a half beat late but at least, Reed told himself, he'd come in at all.

I wanna get away from this place,
I wanna blow my brain, forget your face—

No one had even noticed they were playing again. By the light of the moon, Reed could see a horde of seniors milling about, making out, and lighting things on fire. Up front, next to the platform they'd put together for their stage, their single groupie danced by herself, flinging her tattoo-covered arms in the air in a wild frenzy, despite the slow and moody beat of the music. That was their audience: One goth girl who hated their music but had a not-so-secret crush on Hale.

Reed didn't care.

Same as you always were
Too good too much too fast too far,
And all the knives into my head and all
The holes and all the time to get away—

He knew the lyrics were lame. He didn't care about that, either. The guys all wanted to do cover songs—they'd have wrestling matches over Led Zeppelin versus Coldplay, Bright Eyes versus The Ramones—and then they'd get distracted and Reed would place the only vote that mattered. They played his music. And when he was really in the zone, it was a better high than pot. It was just him and the words and the music. It was cool.

He wasn't in the zone.

And he couldn't stop scanning the crowd.

I wanna get away from this place,

SLOTH

I wanna choke it up and spit in your face—

He stopped singing and held his breath. She was walking through the crowd, which seemed to part slightly as she passed. Her back was to the stage. Her movements were graceful and deliberate, her body slim and perfect. Her sleek black hair spun in the wind as she turned around, and he was about to whisper her name when—

It wasn't her. Of course.

He hadn't believed it, not really, he told himself. But he had. Just for a second, he'd let himself forget—he'd let himself believe that, somehow, it could be her.

"Awesome set!" Fish cried, slamming his stick against one of the cymbals. "Break time."

"Set?" Reed asked, trying to remember himself. "We haven't even gotten through one song."

"Dude, who's fault is that?" Hale asked, giving Reed a pointed look. (As pointed as a look could be when his eyes were half shut.) "I say break time. I've got . . ." He glanced offstage, where goth girl had stripped off her T-shirt to reveal a black leather bikini. She slowly licked her hand, from her palm up to her fingertips, then threw it to Hale as if it were a kiss. "I got stuff to do, kid." Hale ditched the guitar and hopped off the platform, grabbing goth girl and kissing her like he was trying to Hoover her mouth right off her face.

Reed turned to exchange a glance with Fish, but the drummer had already laid his head down on the snare drum and shut his eyes. So much for the gig.

Reed stumbled off the makeshift stage and began to walk without a direction in mind. This wasn't his scene.

Some asshole in a letter jacket with a squealing girl slung over his shoulder slammed into him with a glare and a warning. "Watch it, loser!"

Definitely not his scene.

He was well away from the party and halfway to his car when he realized that he wasn't alone. He didn't turn around to see who was following him, figuring that whoever it was would eventually reveal themselves or, preferably, lose interest and wander away.

It took about five minutes.

"Reed?" Her voice was tentative and musical.

He turned around. "Hey." She looked good. Reed hated himself for noticing.

"Leaving?" Beth asked. "It's early."

"Yeah." He shrugged. "I'm just . . ." He wasn't leaving. He had a tent and a sleeping bag in the truck, and he had a plan. He and the guys were going to hike out to somewhere quiet and alone and have a party of their own. But the guys were useless. ". . . you know."

"Yeah." Beth gave him a wry smile. "This isn't really my thing either."

"Really?" She was too blond and beautiful not to be one of *those* girls.

"I hate parties." There was a pause, though not an awkward one. "I guess I'm going too."

"Unless—" He wanted to be alone. But even with her there, he felt alone—in a good way. He didn't have to put on a show. And maybe—he remembered her tears, and the way she'd shaken in his arms—maybe there were some things she could understand. "You want to hang? You know, just for a while?"

Her eyebrows crinkled together, and there was another pause. Maybe she was trying to decide if he was good enough for her, or what the odds were of anyone seeing them together. Reed decided to forget the whole thing. But she spoke before he could. "Yeah. Okay. Let's, uh . . . hang."

"Cool," he said, wondering if that unclenching in his shoulder blades was relief.

"Cool."

"Baby, you are *so hot!*" the guy said, nuzzling his greasy head into Harper's chest. Harper's head lolled back, her eyes half closed. The guy's fingers crept up her thigh and across her stomach and, encountering no resistance, began to unbutton her shirt. "I mean, *damn!*" he exclaimed, catching his first glimpse of her bare cleavage and pale, creamy skin. "Makes me wanna—"

"Hold that thought," Kane drawled, clamping an iron grip around the guy's scrawny shoulders and tossing him away. "We'll get back to you."

"What's it to you?" the loser whined, trying to elbow Kane out of the way. "Jealous? She wants *me.*"

Kane looked down at Harper, sitting cross-legged on the ground, slumped over at the waist now that there was no one left propping her up, her tangled hair falling over her face. She looked limp and pliable, like a doll that would be content however you posed her.

"She doesn't know what she wants," Kane murmured, then turned toward the greasy loser and smiled. He didn't need to raise a fist to convey his warning. "You should probably get out of here, asshole. *Now.*"

Kane could have taken the guy in a fight, but he knew

it would never come to that. Even a loser like this knew that Kane had all the power, and knew better than to stick around.

"You okay, Grace?" Kane asked, hauling her up. She lifted her head and scowled.

"What are you doing?" she asked, her voice slurred.

"Rescuing you, in case you hadn't noticed."

She shook him away. "I don't need rescuing. I was fine."

"Yeah, you and Drunky McDateRapist were having a grand old time."

"I can hook up with whoever I want."

"Your warm gratitude means the world to me," he said dryly. This knight-in-shining-armor business didn't come with many perks. Probably a good thing: A few more good deeds and his rep would end up in the toilet.

Standing up and arguing seemed to revive her a bit, because the color seeped back into her face and her hand suddenly squeezed down on his. "Let's go!" she cried.

A manic-depressive drunk. Great. *Party on, Kane,* he thought sourly, wondering if it was sexist to believe girls couldn't hold their liquor. Not that he wasn't already an unapologetic sexist—he just liked to be consistent. "Go where?" he asked wearily.

"Dance!" she tugged him toward the whirling crowd, thrashing her head in time to the tinny hip-hop bursting from some cheap speakers. "Come on."

"I don't dance," he reminded her, reluctant to leave her alone again. "How about we go visit your good friend Miranda. She's just over—"

"Shut up and dance with me," she said, threading a finger through his belt loop and pulling him toward her. She ignored the pulsing beat and instead collapsed into his arms, hanging around his neck and swaying back and forth. "Stop rescuing me," she said, her voice muffled by his shirt.

"Stop screwing up," he suggested.

She dragged herself up a few inches and propped her chin up against his chest so that, when he looked down at her, their lips nearly met. "I know what you want," she said, too loudly, a harsh smile twisting her face.

"A private jet? A harem? My own private island?"

"Stop!" she cried, hitting against his chest.

"Stop what?"

"Being nice to me."

Kane tilted his head down enough that their foreheads touched. "I'm never nice. You know that."

Before he knew what was happening, she'd pushed herself up on her toes and kissed him, her hands tightening around his neck. A soft moan escaped her as she pulled away.

"Now I know you're drunk," he joked, his mouth on autopilot as he struggled to plot his next move.

"Shut up," she murmured, kissing his chest, sucking on the bare skin at the nape of his neck.

"You don't know what you're doing, Grace," he warned her, halfheartedly trying to push her away.

"Who cares?" And then her lips were on his again, her tongue probing, her hands massaging his back and then slipping beneath his shirt and clawing against his skin.

If he were a cartoon character, this is the point at which the tiny angel and devil would pop into existence, one perched on each shoulder.

Angel, complete with halo and miniature golden harp: *She's drunk. She's self-destructive. She's out of her mind.*

Devil, with red horns and a familiar smirk: *She's drunk. You're drunk. Let's party. It's all good.*

Angel: *She doesn't really want you.*

Devil: *Everyone wants you. Don't be stupid.*

Angel: *Don't be evil.*

Devil, jabbing him with his tiny pitchfork: *Don't forget about that tight ass, and her magic fingers crawling down toward your waistband, and—is that a black thong peeking out over her jeans?*

Angel: *Ohhh, definitely a thong. And that ass . . .*

Devil: *Told you so.*

Angel: *And that thing she's doing with your ear?*

Devil: *Do they give gold medals for tongue aerobics?*

Angel, slapping the devil five: *God, she's good.*

Devil: *Hallelujah.*

Kane groaned, half in pleasure and half in torture, as he wrestled with himself (and with Harper). And while he deliberated, she kissed him, and groped him, and he let it happen, their bodies tangling together and his mind's voice growing quieter and quieter, drowned in the force of desperate, physical need.

He'd push her away.

He would.

In a minute.

Miranda wandered unsteadily through the crowd. At least the world had stopped spinning and her head had stopped throbbing. But as her mind and vision cleared, she'd realized she was sitting alone on a rock, waiting for someone who, apparently, wasn't coming back.

She was still drunk enough to go and look for him.

First she flipped open her pocket-size mirror and checked things out. Eye shadow a little smeared, mascara intact, fresh coat of "Midnight Rose"-colored lipstick in hopes of looking extra kissable, and she was ready to go.

He wasn't hanging with the stoners, who were sprawled on their backs, passing around a massive bong.

He wasn't, thank god, groping the cheerleaders or charming the prom committee.

He wasn't wandering along the edges of the crowd, looking for her.

He wasn't by the keg, or the speakers, or the jocks, or the trees.

And then time stopped.

She didn't see it as a fluid series of events, but rather as a series of frozen snapshots, flashing in front of her eyes and then fading away:

Kane's back, and a girl's arms roaming across it.

Curly auburn hair falling across a shoulder.

Two faces in profile, eyes closed, tongues locked.

Harper, her eyes open, locked on Miranda. Her smile.

Harper turning away, kissing him again.

Miranda sat down where she'd been standing, Harper and Kane fading from view. All she could see now were people's legs and feet, some walking, some dancing, some standing around, some wrapped up in others. She tried to catch her breath.

She's drunk, Miranda told herself. *Self-destructive. She doesn't know what she's doing.*

But Harper had stopped. Looked at Miranda. Smiled and turned away. She knew exactly what she was doing.

Miranda suddenly felt completely sober and clear. But

she couldn't have been, or she wouldn't have stood up and walked purposefully off toward the crops of Joshua trees, where she'd seen half the basketball team breaking bottles and doing keg stands. If she wasn't drunk, where did she get the nerve to wrap her arms around Adam and whisper in his ear, "I need you, now"?

She didn't think about the consequences or fear humiliation. She just acted, tugging him away from the group, deeper into the trees. She didn't need to think. She'd come to this party to give in to her desires. At the time, those had been: longing, lust, hope.

Now they'd been replaced with one: revenge. She didn't pause to acknowledge that to herself or explain it to Adam. She didn't even need to take a deep breath before kissing him. And she had to admit that Harper had been right. The chiseled face and perfect body was a definite turn-on. As was the prospect of smashing Harper's heart to pieces.

"Miranda?" Adam was out of it, completely, his face slack and his words thick. "Whuh?"

"This doesn't have to mean anything," she said, stripping off her shirt. "It's just for fun." She tugged at the edge of his shirt and stumbled against him. "It's a party, right?"

Adam didn't say anything. But he let her tug him down to the ground, and he didn't resist as she ran her fingers through his hair. She didn't know how to seduce someone, or how to follow up the first move with a second one. *Harper* would know.

Harper was probably doing it right now.

She lay down on her side, ignoring the sharp edges digging into her. "Come here," she told Adam, hooking her finger into his collar and jerking him toward her.

He toppled over with a grunt, then rolled to face her. "Miranda, I'm not really—"

"You waiting around for Harper?" she snapped, enjoying his wince. Suddenly it seemed like the whole world should share in her pain. *See? I can be just like you,* she told Harper silently. *I can be cold, and I can take what you want.* "She's with Kane. Déjà vu all over again, right?"

"Shuddup."

"Kane gets everything, and you get—"

"Shut up." Louder this time.

"Make me," Miranda challenged, jerking her face toward his. Their noses bumped, and then awkwardly but without hesitation, their lips met.

His face was stubbly and his hair too short. His breath was sour, his kiss was rough, angry, but at least she had *acted*. And her eyes were dry. He grunted like an animal, and she accidentally bit his tongue, and the rocks beneath them felt like they were drawing blood. But she persevered. She closed her eyes, kissed him harder, and tried not to pretend he was someone else.

Beth drew in a breath and tried not to cough out the smoke. "This is harder than it looks," she sputtered, lying back against the sleeping bag.

"You'll get the hang of it," Reed assured her. He lay down next to her, and for a long time all she could hear was their breathing, and the whistling of the wind. "You feeling anything?" he asked.

"I don't know . . ." The words sounded strange, and *felt* strange, as if her tongue had suddenly doubled in size. She stuck it out at him. "Does my tongue look weird?" (This came out sounding more like, "Doz ba tog look eered?") She burst into giggles before he could answer.

"Yeah, you're feeling it," he said, satisfied.

Beth waved her hand in front of her face, marveling at the fact that it was too dark to see. *Maybe I don't have a hand anymore,* she thought. *Maybe I'm just a mind.* The theory seemed startlingly profound, and she was about to explain it to Reed, but the words slipped away from her.

"I never knew why she was with me, you know?" His words seemed like they were dropping out of the sky, unconnected to either of them. "I mean, I'm . . . and she was . . . yeah. Like the way she talked. It was like everything she said came out of a book. Like . . ."

Beth zoned out, just listening to the pleasant rise and fall of his voice, tuning for scattered words and phrases— "never again"; "in the water"; "can't stop"; "sundress"; "going crazy"; and, several times, "why"—but she couldn't focus enough to draw them together into a single thread. Every time she tried, she would realize that the ground was hard and soft at the same time, or that the air tasted like peppermint, and she would wander off into her head.

Until it occurred to her: Maybe he was onto her. Maybe he knew her secret. He knew exactly what she'd done, and what she was hiding, and this was his way of torturing her. Beth jerked herself upright and curled her legs up to her chest, trying to catch her breath. He would pretend to be nice to her, and then, just when she felt safe, he would bring the cage down, trap her in her lies, and destroy her. Which was what she deserved. And of course he hated her. She tried to look at his expression, to see if she could find the hatred in his eyes, but it was too dark. She didn't know what he was thinking, but what if he knew what *she* was thinking? The truth was so obvious, he must know. He must be waiting, biding his time, and then—

"Hey." His hand was on her back. His voice didn't sound angry. "What is it?"

"Nothing," she said quickly, gasping for breath. Would he hear the lies in her voice? "I have to get out of here." Away from him.

She tried to stand up, but he stopped her. "Chill. Wait," he urged. "It's not real, whatever it is. It's just the weed. It's just something that happens." He rubbed her back, and she bent her head to her knees. "Deep breaths," he advised, rubbing her back. "Slow, deep breaths."

"I know you know," she said feverishly. "I know you know I know you know you know you know . . ." She repeated the words so many times, they lost all meaning and became absurd, like a made-up language. "Owyoo no new oh," she said experimentally. It suddenly seemed ridiculous that some noises had so much meaning and others were just noise. "New yo I you?" she asked, bursting into laughter as Reed gaped at her in confusion.

Words were so weird.

"Weird," she said, testing out the sound. "Weeeeeeeeeird."

Reed shook his head, bemused. "Yes, you are."

She lay down again on her back, her breathing slowed and her mind clear. Just like the stars, which seemed so bright, like they were holes in the sky. The desert was cold, and empty, but she didn't feel alone. Even though she couldn't see him, she knew he was there.

The world seemed so huge, and so small at the same

time, like she and Reed were the only things in existence. And wouldn't everything be so much easier if that were true. The world felt fresh. The sharp wind against her face, the rough polyester beneath her. Reed's hand brushing, just slightly, against hers—she'd never felt so *there*.

"Are you happy?" she asked.

"No. You?"

"No. But—" She searched for the words that described how she *did* feel, a certainty that she'd never be happy combined with a strange acceptance and even contentment, as if she was floating along and the current was strong but she could trust where it would take her, so she could just close her eyes, sink back, and relax. She felt like she understood everything at once, with a deep clarity— but when she tried to name it, assign words and sentences to the certainty, it flowed away. The closer she drew, the blurrier it got. So she gave up. "But it's okay," she concluded simply.

She heard Reed take a sharp, deep breath and let it out slowly. "Yeah. It's okay. Everything is."

10

"Uhhhhhhhhhhhhh." Miranda opened her eyes. Her first mistake. The morning light burned.

She twisted her head to the left. Mistake number two. The world spun, her stomach lurched, her muscles screamed. Her cottonmouth filled with the sour taste of bile.

Better not to move.

Go slow, she warned herself. Focused on taking one breath, then another, tried to ignore the throbbing pain in her head. *Take stock:*

Arms and legs: fully functional. Too heavy to move.

Location: burning white sun, jagged rocks digging into her back. So, outside. Somewhere, for some reason.

Miscellaneous: Shirt on the ground. Bra unhooked. Her left arm squashed between her chest and the ground, her right arm propped up on something. Something that moved.

Uh-oh.

Her breathing was like thunder in her ears. She held it. The roaring stopped. And she heard him.

She twisted her head around. "Oooooooooooh noooooooo." A weak and scratchy wheeze, but still too loud. She winced. He woke.

"Unnnh?" Adam shook his head and propped himself up, then dropped back down to the ground. "What am I . . . what are you . . . ?"

There was a party, Miranda remembered. Images floated across her brain.

Beer. Lots of beer.

Kane's arms holding her up.

More beer.

Kane and . . . A sharp pain cut through the dull throbbing in her head. *Harper.*

The trees. Adam. Unbuttoning her shirt. His tongue . . .

"What did I do?" she whispered. Her throat burned. "Adam," she croaked. His eyes had slipped shut again. His chest was bare. "Adam!"

"Uh?"

Her arm was still lying on top of him. She jerked it away, heaved herself over onto her back. "Do you remember what . . . what did we . . ." *No. Not possible.* She closed her eyes. *No, no, no. Maybe.* She had to know.

"Did we . . ."

". . . you know?"

Shut up, he thought. Her voice hurt. Everything hurt. Every noise was another bottle broken over his head. And hangovers turned him into an asshole.

Home. That was what he needed. His bed. His dark

room. His Ultimate Hangover Cure (milk, orange juice, honey, bananas). Just what the doctor ordered. But that would mean standing up, and he was too tired to move.

And then there was Miranda. Who wouldn't shut up.

"Adam, what *happened*?"

Be nice. "Okay, okay," he groaned. "Just stop yelling. We kissed, okay?"

"And?"

"And that's it." Adam opened his eyes again. Her lower lip wobbled, and her eyes bugged out. He sighed. "And then you, uh, kind of puked. A lot."

"Oh, god. On you?"

"Well . . ." He took a big whiff. Almost choked. Yeah, on him. He forced a smile. "No big deal. Really."

"This is so humiliating," Miranda moaned, turning away from him and curling up into a tight ball.

"It's fine." *Comfort her,* he told himself. But that would take so much damn effort. He stifled a yawn. "It's already forgotten."

"We can't tell anyone."

"Yeah."

"Promise," Miranda insisted.

"Uh-huh. I promise." He stretched out, feeling like he hadn't moved in months. "We should probably get going."

"Yeah."

Minutes passed. No one spoke. No one moved.

"Or we could just rest for a while," Miranda suggested. But no one heard. Adam was already asleep.

"Uhhhhhhhhhhhhhh." Beth opened her eyes. Her whole body ached. The thin sleeping bag offered no protection for her from the hard-packed desert gravel. She was tired. Thirsty.

Happy.

My parents are going to kill me.

It didn't seem to matter.

Maybe the pot permanently warped my brain. Maybe I just don't care anymore.

It sounded like heaven.

She had awoken in the night, shivering in the dark. Reed had wrapped an arm around her; she'd snuggled up against his chest. Now she could feel him breathe.

She felt like a stranger. And it felt good. As long as she stayed out here, she could be someone else. She could be the kind of girl who didn't care what happened next.

"Reed?" Her head was nestled into the space beneath his chin. He didn't answer, and she couldn't see his face.

The calm couldn't last forever. But maybe when he woke up, he'd pull out his small plastic bag again. He'd roll the ashy, dark green flakes into a neat white tube. She would inhale more of the magic potion.

I shouldn't . . .

It was a quiet voice, and easy to ignore. To smother, until it stopped flailing and gave up the fight.

She closed her eyes and shifted against him. It felt good—a warm body beside her, the weight of someone's arms around her. She'd been so alone.

She knew she deserved to be alone.

But in the sunrise, in the desert air, in Reed's arms, she could almost allow herself to forget.

"I wish I could tell you the truth," she whispered as he slept. "I wish we could stay here forever."

❖❖❖

I have to get out of here, Reed thought. He squeezed his eyes shut. *Don't speak. Don't move.* If she knew he was awake, she'd want to talk. And he wasn't ready.

So he pretended to be asleep. He pretended to be somewhere else. Not here, lying next to *her*, with his arms around her, breathing in her hair, wishing he could—

Stop.

He wasn't betraying Kaia. Nothing had happened. Nothing had to happen. It was innocent.

But didn't he want more?

Didn't he like the way her body felt against his?

He was comfortable with Beth, safe. He could *talk* to her—in a way he'd never talked to Kaia.

That was the betrayal.

I miss her, he said silently, as he did every morning. And every morning, he woke up with a hole inside of him. Feeling like if he looked down he would see that a part of his chest was just missing, or that his legs had suddenly become transparent. He felt unwhole.

Except that this morning, he didn't.

It didn't feel like Kaia was watching, or that he could ask for forgiveness. She felt far away, like someone he'd imagined. Reed wanted to push Beth aside, stand up, brush off all traces of her, and leave her behind as he drove home, alone. And Reed always did exactly what he wanted.

He kept still. He kept silent. He stayed.

"Uhhhhhhhhhhhhhh." Some asshole was trying to wake her. She'd kick his ass. Except that would mean sitting up.

"Time to get up, Sleeping Beauty," Kane said, standing

up and dumping her to the ground. She'd fallen asleep sitting up, leaning against his shoulder, and now she found herself facefirst in the dirt. Asshole was right.

"Aren't you supposed to wake me with a kiss?" Harper groaned.

"I would think you had enough of that last night."

"Uch." Harper spat into the dirt. "Don't remind me."

"Glad to know it was as good for you as it was for me," Kane said dryly, sitting down again, a safe distance away.

Harper stayed where she was. She remembered everything. Unfortunately. "Don't be bitter just because you didn't get anything more than a kiss," she chided him. "I'm sure you'll get over it, in time."

Kane snorted. "I'm the one who pushed *you* away, lovergirl. Or have you forgotten, 'Kane, I want you! I need you! Give it to me now!'?" he asked, affecting a high, nasal voice.

"I did *not*," Harper said indignantly.

"You tell yourself whatever you need to get by, dearest—we both know what really happened." Kane yawned and pulled a small flask out of his pocket. He took a gulp. "Hair of the dog. Want some?" She waved it away. "How do you feel?" he asked in a softer voice.

Physically, she felt fine.

"I feel like shit," she said, curling up and burying her head in her arms. "Like somebody flushed me down the toilet and I ended up lying in a puddle of crap at the bottom of the sewer system."

In other words, same as always. But he didn't need to know that.

"I'm just going to go back to sleep," she lied, closing

her eyes. That was the answer. She'd escape into the hangover. She wouldn't have to talk, she wouldn't have to smile. She could just be—and be miserable.

Her voice faded, and she was out. Kane rolled his eyes. He was wide awake, despite the fact that he'd been sitting up most of the night. Not to keep an eye on her, he told himself. Just because how the hell was he supposed to sleep sitting up, leaning against a giant, lumpy rock, with a girl passed out on top of him.

And not even a real girl—just Harper.

She was a mess. Not that she'd ever admit it. She wasn't a whiner; she didn't cry and cling to you like she'd fall down if you weren't there to hold her up. She'd rather crash.

And let him pick up the pieces.

No one had made him stay, of course. No one was making him stay now. And no one had made him untangle himself from a horny Harper and sit her down on the rocks, forcing her to calm down and stop groping him. He'd ditched the action to tend to her, keeping her out of trouble and pretending he didn't notice her tears. And he had no one to blame but himself.

It was the party of the year, and he'd spent the whole thing tending to drunken *friends*. Being *solicitous*. Exercising *restraint*.

Kane didn't do hangovers. But the thought of all that wasted potential was enough to make him sick.

chapter

11

Achy and bleary-eyed, Beth stepped through her front door—and into an ambush.

"Where the hell have you been?"

"Are you okay?"

"What were you thinking?"

"Why didn't you call?"

Beth sighed, ducked her head, and waited for the yelling to stop.

"Well?" Her father loomed over her, fuming, while her mother slumped onto the frayed living-room couch, her eyes rimmed with red. Beth supposed she should feel sorry for causing concern, but all she had to offer was surprise and a mild disgust.

"Well what?" she asked. "I told you I was going to a party. I stayed over."

Her father's eyes widened. She knew what they'd been expecting. Sweet, mild-mannered Beth, always responsible and always apologetic. She was sick of it.

"Do you know how we felt when we woke up and saw you never came home last night?" her father boomed. "Do you know what we thought?"

"That you'd actually have to make your own breakfast for once?" Beth snapped, horrified as soon as the words popped out of her mouth. But there was no taking them back, and she didn't particularly want to.

"*What did you say?*"

"You heard me."

"Beth, Beth, sweetie." Her mother shook her head sorrowfully, giving Beth her well-practiced martyr look. "Things around here are hard enough without . . . we really expected more of you."

Beth wanted to kick something. "Too bad!" she cried, all the stress of the last week shooting out of her. "I'm *seventeen*, Mom. I'm not your maid, I'm not your babysitter, I'm not your cook, I'm your *daughter*, and sometimes I screw up. *Deal with it.*"

"That's it!" her father shouted. "Go up to your room. Your mother and I don't have time to deal with your temper tantrum right now."

Cue the guilt: Her parents both worked triple shifts and were constantly exhausted. The twins took a lot of work. The house was always a mess. It was Beth's responsibility to pitch in and shut up. She knew all that—but today, she just didn't care.

"I'm out of here," she muttered, turning her back on her parents.

"Don't you disobey me," her father warned. "Get back here."

"Or what?" Beth kept her back to him, not wanting

him to see the tears threatening to spill out of her eyes. "You'll punish me? You'll disown me? If it turns out I'm not one hundred percent perfect, you'll just stop loving me?"

"Beth, what are you—?" Her mother's voice broke. Beth forced herself not to give in to the inevitable tears. She slipped out the door before her father could issue any more threats or her mother any pleas.

I'm not who they think I am, she told herself, getting into the car without knowing where to go next. *Better they find that out now.*

Tyson versus Holyfield.

Bush versus Gore.

Jennifer versus Angelina.

As all-time grudge matches go, they had nothing on this.

In one corner: Miranda Sellers, five feet of fighting force powered by jealousy, humiliation, a world-class hangover, two months of repressed anger, and eighteen years of repressed everything else.

In the other corner: the undefeated champion Harper Grace, aka the Terminator, aka the Beast, aka the Ice Queen, who would settle for nothing less than unconditional surrender.

Ladies, come out fighting—and try to keep this fair and above the belt.

As if.

Miranda and Harper circled each other warily, each waiting for the other to land the first blow. Harper had the home-court advantage, which only meant that she had nowhere to escape. Miranda had shown up at her door, dragged Harper up to her bedroom, and now, behind closed doors and with a bleary-eyed ferocity, was ready to pounce. On the wall behind her hung a bulletin board covered in photos of the dynamic duo's greatest hits: junior high dances, makeover-themed slumber parties, crappy double dates, and triumphant after-parties. It was a vivid documentary record of their friendship; but at the moment, it was irrelevant.

Miranda swung first. "How could you?" she asked, pacing around Harper in a tight circle.

"What?"

"I saw you with Kane," Miranda snapped. "It was disgusting."

"So?"

"So you know how I feel about him."

Harper landed the first blow. She laughed. "So maybe I don't care."

"That's obvious," Miranda retorted. "You don't care about anything."

Point to Miranda.

"What do you know?" Harper yelled, her face turning red.

"Nothing!" Miranda shouted back. "Because you won't *let* me!" She paused, and sucked in a lungful of air. "I'm supposed to be your best friend," she said quietly.

Harper threw her hands in the air. "Since when? Last month you hated me, this month you love me. Gosh," she said sarcastically, opening her eyes wide in confusion. "I just can't keep track."

"Last month you screwed me over and were a total bitch about it!" Miranda snapped. "This month . . ."

"Yeah." Harper scowled. "This month you're back, because you feel sorry for me. Like I need that!"

The gloves were off.

Miranda wanted to cry. But, instead, she balled up her fists, wishing she could land a real blow.

Harper felt the anger explode from her, and it was such a blissful release to finally let it go that she didn't care who was in the line of fire. She didn't care who she was really angry at—Miranda was there, and she made for an easy target. It just felt so good, after all these weeks, to shout, to scream, to unclench her muscles, to drop the fake smile.

To let herself *feel*.

It was almost worth it.

Even when Miranda pounded her fist against the wall, slammed through the door, and left Harper alone.

Here is what Miranda remembered as she walked down the driveway to her car, trying to keep her face turned away from Adam's house, and trying not to cry:

The sneer on Harper's face and the ice in her eyes.

The sound of Harper laughing at her pain.

And, most of all, Harper's words.

"Maybe if you weren't so goddamn annoying and in my face *all! The! Time!*"

"Stop pretending you can understand anything about me!"

"I don't need your pity and I don't need you!"

And here is what Harper remembered as she sat on the edge of her bed and let the numbness seep back in:

Miranda's eyes blinking back tears.

Miranda's voice shaking as she spit out everything she'd been holding back.

Miranda's attack, the words they both knew were true.

"Why is everything always about *you*?"

"Of course I felt sorry for you—why else would I pretend you weren't such a bitch?"

"I've been your best friend for ten fucking years—you barely even *knew* her!"

Mostly, both girls remembered the end.

"You want to be miserable? You want to be totally self-destructive and pathetic and blow off anyone who tries to help?" Miranda asked, disgusted. "Don't let me stop you."

Harper opened her bedroom door and waved her hand like an usher. "Don't let *me* stop *you* from leaving."

And with that, they were both down for the count.

Reed was on his back under the truck, monkeying with the exhaust system, when she came into the garage. He could only see her feet and ankles: thin, black pumps with a low heel; pale, delicate ankles growing from them, narrow enough that he could probably encircle each with one hand. He'd seen those feet before.

"Hello? Is anybody here? Hello?"

For a moment, Reed considered hiding under the truck until she gave up and went away. And he might have, if his wrench hadn't slipped out of his fingers and clattered to the floor. After that, he had no choice.

He wheeled himself out from under the truck and sat up, wiping his greasy hands against his jeans. Beth was still wearing the same outfit she'd worn the night before. It had looked perfect at the party; here, surrounded by chains and toolboxes and busted carburetors, it didn't fit.

"What's up?" he asked, not really wanting to know.

Her face was flushed and tearstained, and her hands kept flickering toward her head. She would twirl a strand of hair, tuck it behind her ears, put her arm down, and then, a moment later, start twirling again, as if she couldn't help herself. "I didn't know where else to go," she said simply. "I thought . . ."

She looked so lost and fragile, he just wanted to go to her and hug her. He wanted to fix her problem, whatever it was.

But why? he asked himself. *What's she to you?*

"Can we, uh, go somewhere?" Beth asked, her lip trembling.

Reed shook his head. "I got a lot of stuff to do here," he said. "You know."

"Maybe I could just hang out for a while?" she asked, almost pleading. "I really just need—"

"No." It would be too easy to be happy if she were there. And he shouldn't be happy, not with someone else. "I told you, I've got stuff to do. You'd be in the way."

"Oh." She looked like he'd punched her. "Okay." She began backing out of the garage, her eyes whipping back and forth, searching fruitlessly for something to focus on. "See you around, I guess."

He shrugged. "Maybe. Whatever."

Then she was gone. He felt like an asshole. And he hurt.

He hadn't lit up since the night before, and now, as the pain crept back into his brain, seemed like as good a time as any. He grabbed his stash out of the glove compartment and wandered outside, sitting on a small ledge behind the garage. He'd have plenty of privacy.

It was a familiar, soothing routine, parsing it out, rolling it up, sealing the blunt with a swift and smooth flick of the tongue.

A few deep breaths and he'd be able to float away, beyond all the pain and all the shit. It would stop hurting.

Reed brought the joint to his lips—and stopped.

He still missed Kaia when he was high. It was a dull, faint throbbing, like a bruise that's turned invisible but has yet to fully heal. Not like now, when the pain was sharp and clear.

The pain was the only thing that was clear, and it burned everything else away. Maybe instead of putting the fire out, this time he should let it burn. He hadn't cried when Kaia died, or yelled or pounded his fist into a glass window, as he'd wanted. He had just smoked up, and that made it all go away.

Just as he'd made Beth go away.

Reed didn't know why he couldn't let her get close.

He didn't know why he couldn't forget the touch of Kaia's fingers on his neck—but could no longer picture her face.

He didn't know if there was some time limit on what he felt, if one day he'd wake up and things would be right again—and he didn't know what he was supposed to do if that never happened.

He stuffed the joint into one pocket, and the plastic bag into another. He was tired of being confused. Maybe, just for a while, he'd stay clear. It was worth a try. And if it was too much, relief was no more than a few lungfuls away.

In the back of Miranda's closet, behind the stash of liquor, cigarettes, old issues of *Cosmo*, and a single pack of condoms that she enjoyed owning but had no expectation of using anytime soon, there was a stack of cardboard boxes. There were seven of them, each labeled in black permanent marker; one for each year, stretching back to sixth grade, and one extra for everything that had come before.

Every year, Miranda set aside an empty desk drawer and filled it with all the detritus of life that most normal people threw out. When the year ended, she dumped the contents into a box and started her collection over again. There were the obvious—ticket stubs, photographs, birthday cards—but everyone with the slightest pack rat tendency saved those. Miranda had an eye for the more subtle mementos: take-out menus, empty cigarette boxes, fliers for concerts she'd never attended, notes passed in class, detention slips, matchbooks, napkins, receipts, anything that might someday bring faded memories back to full color. Her mother liked to call her "the connoisseur of crap," but as Miranda saw it, she was curating the museum of her life.

It was a narrow life, she saw now, sitting on the floor surrounded by half-open boxes and carefully sorted mounds of memories. There was the occasional homemade Valentine's Day card from her little sister, and an entry pass left over from a long-ago family trip to some amusement park that had gone bankrupt only a few months later. But those were the exception; Harper was the rule.

Item: a torn scrap of lined paper, with the initials HG and SP written in neon, encircled by a light blue heart. (Pink had been out that year.) Harper had slipped Miranda the note while their sixth-grade teacher, Ms. Hernandez, had droned on and on about Lewis and Clark. Miranda knew exactly what it meant. For weeks, Harper had been drooling over

Scott Pearson, universally acknowledged to be the cutest boy in the sixth grade, except for Craig Jessup, who didn't count because he smelled like mildew. Everyone knew that Scott had been planning to take Harper behind the school at recess, and kiss her. They'd disappeared after lunch, right on schedule—and now they were back in the classroom, and here was Harper's note. Miranda got the story on the walk home: He'd kissed her. It was wet, and sloppy, and gross, and now he was her boyfriend. Miranda made Harper promise to tell her every detail of everything that happened, so that she, too, could know what having a boyfriend was like. And Harper came through, recounting every moment she spent with Scott for the nine days their relationship lasted. Then Scott moved on to Leslie Giles, a seventh grader with bigger boobs, and Harper pretended her heart was broken, to get sympathy from every girl in school. Only Miranda got to hear the dirty little secret: Scott had bad breath, kissing was boring, and she was glad to be done with the whole stupid thing.

Item: a wrinkled napkin from High Score, a sports bar that had closed a couple years ago, probably because its TV was only thirty-two inches wide and its waitresses, who mostly looked like they'd been around since the Eisenhower administration, preferred using it to catch up on SOAPnet reruns of *Dynasty* and *Melrose Place*. For her sixteenth birthday, Harper had given Miranda her very first fake ID. It was crude and cheap, and claimed Miranda was a twenty-one-year-old Virginian named Melanie DeWitt, born May 27, Gemini, residing on Applewood Road, Manassas, Virginia, 20108. All details Miranda had struggled to memorize before they set out to test her new identity at

High Score, where it was reputed that they'd let in a second grader if she flashed a homemade library card with her picture taped to it. Miranda was still nervous, forcing Harper to give her a pep talk before they strutted past the bouncer, flashing their ridiculous IDs, and sat down at a bar together for the first time. And despite the gross tables, nasty smells, and cheap beer, it had been the first truly great night of Miranda's life.

Item: a program from the ninth-grade musical, *Oliver!* Miranda had wanted to try out—and, given the size of their school, "try out" really meant "write your name on the list and Mr. Grady will assign you your part." But Harper had labeled it TLFU, Too Lame For Us. Lots of things were TLFU that year, which, not coincidentally, had marked the beginning of Harper's rise to the top of the social stratosphere. White sneakers, boy bands, binders, the color pink (in the previous year, now out once again), eighth-grade boys, PG movies, sparkly nail polish—all TLFU. It was a lot for Miranda to remember, which was why, as in the case of the school musical, Harper had to keep reminding her. But they'd gone to see it, because Harper had scored them an invitation to the cast party, hosted by geeky Mara Schneider, whose brother Max was a junior and topped the official list of high school hunks. Max was supposed to be at the party, but didn't show. Instead, Harper and Miranda got stuck in a corner with Barry and Brett Schanker. Barry had played the Artful Dodger, Brett had played the trumpet in the pit; both were pale, gangly, pockmarked, and intent on getting Harper and Miranda to play Twister with them in Mara Schneider's rec room. Instead, Harper and Miranda had escaped into the backyard, where they'd spent the night dangling their feet in the Schneiders' pool, smoking a full pack of cigarettes (courtesy of Brett Schanker), getting drunk on the hot pink "Kool-Aid-plus" punch, and pretending that they were the only two people there, or at least the only two who mattered. By the end of the night, Miranda had thrown up in the bushes, Harper had nearly fallen into the pool, and, in an act of mad courage (or courageous madness), they'd snuck up to Max's room and snagged a pair of his boxers. (White, size medium, and covered in bright yellow happy faces; Max, they decided, was definitely TLFU.)

Item: a dried carnation from tenth-grade Valentine's Day, left over from the bouquet Harper had given Miranda when she freaked out about not having a boyfriend.

Item: a magazine clipping of a tropical island, where they'd dreamed of someday co-owning a vacation house with their unspeakably wealthy and unbelievably handsome husbands.

Item: a Scrabble tile, rescued from the trash, after Harper—tired of losing each and every rainy day—had dumped the game.

Item: a thin, green plastic ring purchased for a quarter from a gumball machine. They'd each bought one, pledging to wear them forever. Miranda had lost hers first—this was Harper's, because they both knew that Miranda's cardboard boxes were the only place it would be safe.

Miranda rubbed her eyes. She'd been looking through the boxes for hours, as if something in one of them would be able to explain what was happening. But there were no answers, only the record of a friendship that should have been enough.

It was enough for Miranda—it had, for all these years, been nearly everything, and here was the proof. So why did Harper need so much more? And why was she willing to trash it, for Adam, for Kane, for Kaia, for anything?

Miranda had been willing to put everything aside for Harper's time of need, because that's what best friends do. But it was obvious now: Whatever Harper needed, it wasn't her.

Sometimes, she knew it was a dream while it was happening.

"Where are we?" she asked Kaia, gaping at the tiny huts lining the cobblestone streets. They wound up and around into the hills, giving way to long stretches of emerald green vineyards. On the other side, the land dropped off abruptly, and at the base of a cliff lapped the waters of a calm, turquoise sea.

"Italy," Kaia said, looking bored. She slipped on a pair of sunglasses, despite the cloudy sky. "A little fishing village on the Riviera."

"But I've never been here," Harper said, confused. She'd never been out of California, not that she would have admitted it to Kaia, with her passport stuffed full of stamps from glamorous getaways to international hot spots.

"I have," Kaia said, shrugging. "It gets old."

"But this is *my* dream," Harper pointed out. She wandered down one of the uneven paths, stopping just before the land dropped off to nothingness. Keeping her back to the town and staring out over the cliff face, she felt like she was on the edge of the world. "How can—?"

"You want to argue?" Kaia asked, stretching out on the ground as if she were at the beach. "Or you want to get a tan?"

Harper tossed a small rock over the edge of the cliff. She tried to follow its way down, but didn't see it land. "What are we doing here? What are *you* doing here? You're . . ."

"Can't say it, can you?" Kaia laughed bitterly. "Dead. Kaput. Kicked the bucket. Passed over to . . . woooooooh . . ." She made her voice dramatically low and solemn, "the *Other Side.*"

"I was going to say, 'You're *annoying* me,'" Harper corrected her. "Can't you just leave me alone?"

"I did leave you alone. Isn't that the problem?" Kaia stood up and brushed herself off. "Why else are you acting like such a mental case?" Before Harper could answer—not that she had an answer—Kaia wandered over to a small storefront, where she haggled with a stooped old man. She came back a moment later with an ice-cream cone heaped high with dripping scoops of chocolate and handed it to Harper.

"None for you?" Harper asked.

"Some of us actually *care* about our figures," Kaia said, giving Harper a pointed look. She ignored it and took a big, slippery mouthful. It was chilly and delicious and, just like everything else, seemed somehow more real than waking life. For weeks, everything had looked gray, tasted dull; but here, even the air tasted sweet, and the ocean blazed a brilliant blue.

She stared down at the jagged rocks at the base of the cliff. The waves slammed against them, frothy geysers spurting several feet into the air. Harper crept closer to the edge, feeling a strange sense of power and possibility. Taking another step seemed like such a small, routine choice—she took steps every day, thousands of them—but the next one could launch her into midair, hundreds of feet above the ground.

What happens if you die in a dream? she wondered.

And maybe she wouldn't die at all—maybe the water would cushion her and she would float away. Or maybe, since it was a dream, she would step off the ground and discover she could fly.

She was too afraid to find out.

"I don't blame you." Kaia's voice was almost lost in the thunder of the crashing surf.

Harper didn't turn around. It was all so easy for Kaia. It always had been. She just did whatever the hell she wanted, and then walked away. Disappeared. Harper was the one left to face the consequences. Harper was the one left to bear the pain.

She wanted to scream, as loud as she could, to see if her voice could fill the emptiness that lay before her, the vast ocean and sky bleeding together in a field of blue. She wanted to berate Kaia for leaving, to beg her to come back, to admit the horrible truth: More than anything, she wished she and Kaia had never met. Because then this whole nightmare—before the accident, and after—would disappear. But even though it was a dream, that was no excuse to let things get out of control, or to feel the things she wasn't allowed to feel.

She opened her mouth, intending to apologize—for what she'd done, for what she'd thought, for what she'd wished. But something else leaked out.

"Maybe it doesn't matter," she told Kaia in a tight, level voice. "Maybe I blame *you.*"

chapter

12

It turned out school was just as boring when you weren't high.

Reed's experiment was in its fifth day, and so far, so . . . okay. He hadn't had any remarkable revelations; his newly clear mind hadn't discovered the meaning of life or the secrets of cold fusion. (Though it did make it a bit easier for him, in remedial physics, to finally figure out what cold fusion was—school was mildly more informative when you bothered to show up to class, rather than skulk in the parking lot.) He hadn't even decided whether his mind was actually clearer, to be honest. Things seemed to move faster, and matter more, but that just meant that more stuff crowded into his head, none of it making much sense.

Fish and Hale were a bit confused, but when weren't they? And they didn't care what he did. "Whatever, dude" was a one-size-fits-all response.

Reed was beginning to realize that no one much cared what he did. The teachers who ignored his absence didn't perk up at his presence. His father was happy as long as he kept his job and stayed out of jail. Fish and Hale just needed someone to snag them the occasional free pizza. Kaia was gone. And Beth . . .

Beth was avoiding him, her face turning red every time their paths crossed. Not that it happened often; she existed in a different world. Usually, people like her didn't even see him—he was a part of the background, like the garbage cans lining the cafeteria or the gum stuck under every desk.

It was okay with Reed. Being invisible made it easier to watch. He saw Beth hovering on the fringes of crowds, always fidgeting, rarely speaking, never setting off on her own. He watched her spend lunch periods in the library, hunched over a book. Once, he glimpsed her slip away to the newspaper office, her hands covering her eyes to mask the tears.

It seemed like her eyes were always on the verge of filling with tears. But maybe that was just because they were such a shimmering, limpid blue.

He didn't even know why he was watching, until the fifth day, when he made his decision.

He ditched school after lunch—that would give him plenty of time to be back before the final bell. It took him about twenty minutes to drive the familiar route, and with every passing mile, the lump of dread in his stomach grew bigger. But at the same time, the closer he got, the more he needed to be there, and the faster he drove.

Reed pulled off onto the shoulder and stared up at the imposing hulk of a building. He'd brought Kaia here, the first time he'd brought her anywhere, back when he'd thought she was just some stuck-up rich bitch. But she'd understood what he saw in the place, and though she never said it, Reed was sure she felt the same way. They'd come out here a lot, sitting silently, staring at the abandoned machinery, the rusted barbed wire, the gaping maw of the mines themselves, and imagining the past.

He hadn't been back since the accident. And he wouldn't be coming back again. He just needed to say good-bye.

He stepped out of the car and forced himself to stare at the spot of their last night here together, as if he could still see the imprint of his blanket on the ground. It hurt like hell. But that was the point.

After a moment, he tore himself away and headed toward the gap-ridden metal fence that surrounded the heart of the refining complex. Ducking through a huge, jagged hole just to the left of a rusted NO TRESPASSING sign, he emerged in the land of forgotten machines. One of the burned-out buildings was missing a large piece of its wall, allowing him to step inside. He wandered past the towering tubes and smokestacks, skirted the giant husks of machines made for smashing and sifting and smelting and sorting, and tried to pretend the whole place didn't feel like it was about to collapse.

In the middle of the refinery he stopped, turning slowly in place, soaking it in. He wanted to remember every detail. But he barely registered the rusted machinery or the blackened walls. He saw only her face.

The pain hit him, raw and scalding. He couldn't stand to be here, surrounded by her absence. He couldn't even think about the time they'd spent here—because when he thought of her now, all he could picture was a burning heap of metal, a lifeless hand, a wooden cross. Someday, maybe, he'd be able to remember the way she was, not the way she ended up. And then he would want something to remember her by.

Reed knelt to the ground and grabbed the first thing he saw: a thin, curved piece of metal half buried in the ground. Half of it was rusted, but the other half was polished smooth and looked almost new. It was about three inches long and an inch wide, and curved at almost a right angle, one end flaring out into a hollow tube shape and the other rounding to form a small, silver sphere. He clenched it in his fist, enjoying the warmth.

It would make a good souvenir. He walked back to the car, hesitating for a moment before he got inside.

"Good-bye," he said aloud, feeling like an idiot.

I'm not coming back, he said silently, wishing he could believe he wasn't just talking to himself. He gripped the small piece of metal tighter, and the flat end dug sharply into his palm. *But I won't forget.*

Bourquins @ 3?

Miranda hadn't expected the text message and didn't know what to do when it arrived. So she fell back on the default option: Obey Harper.

She hadn't responded, but she'd shown up, arriving a few minutes early so she could grab her coffee and be sitting down if and when Harper arrived. She needn't have bothered; Harper, as always, was late.

Harper didn't bother to stop at the counter; she just came straight to the back corner, where Miranda had snagged a table next to the window. The heavy pink drapes were drawn back, and a splash of sunlight fell across her lap. If they stayed long enough, they'd be able to watch the sunset; it didn't seem likely.

Miranda waited. Harper sat down without saying anything, and for a few moments the two girls just stared at each other. Miranda refused to speak first, no matter how difficult it was to stand the silence.

"So," Harper finally said.

Miranda decided that didn't count, and kept her mouth shut.

After another long pause, Harper rolled her eyes. "Look, I'm sorry. I didn't . . . the thing with Kane, it wasn't . . ."

"So what was it, then?"

Harper shrugged.

"Do you want me to hate you?" Miranda asked—realizing, once the words were out there, that maybe that was exactly it.

Harper looked down at the table. "Do you?" she asked quietly.

Miranda sighed. She scraped her spoon around the bottom of her empty coffee mug, then tapped it a few times against the rim. "No. God, Harp, I love you. Don't you get that?"

Harper didn't look up. She drew her arms close against her body, as if for protection, though Miranda suspected she didn't even realize she was doing it. She held her body rigidly still. She obviously wasn't going to say anything, but Miranda remembered those boxes in the back of her closet, and decided to keep going.

"I'm your best friend," she said simply. "I want to help. I know you don't think I understand, and maybe I don't, but I get that you miss—" Miranda paused. She'd been so wary this month of saying the name by accident, dropping it into concentration and setting off some kind of emotional explosion, that it required a force of will to spit it out now. "*Kaia*. If I don't understand the rest, it's because you don't tell me anything."

Harper was now trembling, and still staring down at the table.

"I can do whatever you need me to do, but you have to *tell* me. Whatever you need, I'm there. But if you don't need me . . ." Miranda took a deep breath. She didn't want to get angry or hysterical—she just needed to get this out so that she would know she'd tried everything she could. "If you want me to stop bothering you, fine. I'll go away. You just—I need to know what you want. Just *say* it."

Harper finally looked up. She took a deep, shuddering breath, opened her mouth, then shut it again.

Long minutes went by, and nothing happened. Miranda shook her head in disgust. She stood up, pushed her chair in, and gave her best friend a curt wave. "See ya."

She'd turned her back and already walked away when Harper finally spoke. "I do . . . I need you."

Miranda turned slowly but didn't come any closer, as if Harper were a wild beast she was liable to frighten away.

"I just need some time, Rand, okay?" Harper was looking down at the table once again, her voice high and tight. "Can you just . . . wait for me?"

It wasn't much, but Miranda suddenly felt weightless. "Sure," she said, trying to sound like the whole thing was no big deal. "And when you're ready—I'll be there."

✧✧✧

The truck skidded to a stop a foot in front of her. Reed's face peered out from the open window. "Get in."

"What?" Beth's mind wasn't at its sharpest these days, and, given that it had been days since she'd expected—and hoped—never to see him again, the scene took a moment to process.

"Get in." He leaned across to the passenger door and pushed it open for her. "Come on, trust me."

Never, Beth thought, in the history of the universe, had the words "trust me" led to anything but disaster. But she didn't have particularly far to fall.

She got in.

"I'm sorry," he said. "About before."

"Okay." She waited for him to elaborate, but he was apparently done talking. Beth shrugged and turned to look out the window as the desert streamed by. They drove for a little under an hour, without conversation or music. Beth closed her eyes, listening to the steady hum of the engine and the snap, crackle, pop of rocks and sticks kicked up by the tires and clattering against the underside of the truck. She'd almost drifted off to sleep when the truck made a sharp turn, swinging off the main highway onto a narrow, bumpy dirt road that seemed to wind into an expanse of nothingness.

Beth wondered if she should be concerned—then closed her eyes again and let the bumping and rocking of the truck guide her back toward sleep.

"We're here," Reed suddenly said, pulling to a stop. He grabbed a couple bottles of water from the back and tossed one to Beth. "Let's go."

They were deep in the desert, standing at the foot of an unnaturally smooth, bright white expanse. A dry lake, Beth realized, as they hiked across—there were a few of them sprinkled across the area, but she'd only ever seen them from a car window. As they crossed the lake, it appeared on the horizon: an enormous cone, hundreds of feet high and wide, spurting out of a field of jagged, reddish-black rock.

"Salina Crater," Reed said, as Beth's eyes widened. "It's prehistoric."

They followed a gently sloping path into the crater's center, climbing over hardened lava rolls and scrambling up a slippery trail toward the top. The afternoon sun beat down on them, and Beth gulped her water greedily, pouring a tiny trickle down the back of her neck. She shivered at the delicious touch of cold. She was breathing too hard to speak, but it didn't matter; the breathtaking size and alien beauty of the place had stolen all her words. It felt like they'd traveled back in time and that, when they emerged at the top of the rim, they would see a panorama of roiling volcanoes and wandering dinosaurs stretched out before them.

There were no dinosaurs, but she still gasped at the view. The white lake stretched out to their left, dwarfing the tiny strip of black that marked the highway, and in the other direction, a range of low, rolling mountains dotted the horizon.

"This is amazing," she breathed. She'd been feeling alone in the world for so long—but now, here, she actually understood what that would mean.

The rim was at least ten feet wide, and Reed sat down

toward the outer edge, gesturing for her to join him.

"I can't believe this place," she said quietly, not wanting to disrupt the absolute calm and stillness of the setting.

"My dad told me about it," Reed said. He should have looked totally out of place up here, in his black, ripped punk rock T-shirt and dark, stained jeans. But somehow, he fit perfectly. "I always wanted to check it out, but just never, you know."

"So why today?" she asked. The sun was dipping toward the horizon, and part of her worried that they should start back down so they wouldn't have to hike in the dark. But she didn't want to go anywhere.

"I wanted to go somewhere new." He chewed on the edge of his thumbnail for a moment, then shook himself. "I wanted to—"

And then his lips brushed against hers, so lightly that, if she'd had her eyes closed, she might have thought she imagined it. They were soft, and tender, and then, before she knew what was happening, they were gone.

"Reed . . ." Beth covered her face with her hands and leaned toward the ground, as if she were praying. What was she supposed to do? Not this—she was certain of that. Not with him.

His hands grabbed hers and gently pried them away from her face.

"You don't even know me," she whispered. "You don't know what I've done."

"I don't care." He was still holding her hands. "Screw the past. We're here, *now*."

"I *want* to tell you . . ." But she knew she couldn't.

"Don't. Let's just . . . be." His lashes were so long, and

dark, like a girl's. And in his eyes, which she'd once thought were a deep brown, she could now see flecks of blue, green, silver, even violet. He was looking at her like he could see into her—like he knew everything.

Of course he didn't.

But maybe he really didn't want to. Maybe they could make a fresh start, and help each other forget the past; or at least move forward.

"Your move," he said, his lips turning up into a half smile.

She moved.

It was the kind of kiss you imagine when you're a kid, dreaming of a fairy tale romance: soft, chaste, quick, and perfect. Beth broke away first. If she was going to do this, she was going to do it slowly.

Reed stood up and took her hand, pulling her off the ground. He led her to the edge of the rim and put his arm around her. She nestled against him, and they stood in silence, watching the sun blaze toward the horizon. The desert stretched on forever, still and silent, miles of emptiness in every direction. It seemed like civilization, and along with it, her life, her problems, and everyone else in the world were just figments of her imagination.

So it was especially strange that, for the first time in months, she felt like she wasn't alone.

Harper huddled under her covers with the phone cradled to her chest for more than an hour before she got up her nerve to call.

He didn't answer, and she almost hung up—but she stopped herself, just in time.

"I know I told you to leave me alone," she said after the beep, talking quickly before she lost her nerve, "but—"

She couldn't say it.

I need you—it wasn't her, no matter how true it might be. "Just come find me when you get this. Please."

She told him where she'd be, and hung up. Her parents, who'd thankfully given up on the nightly family bonding sessions, were downstairs watching TV and would be only too delighted to let her go out and meet a friend for "coffee," even if it was a school night. Harper promised them she'd be home early, then hurried out to the driveway, forcing herself not to look up at Adam's dark and empty bedroom window.

There were no lights on the road, and she had some trouble finding the right spot, but the thin white cross glowed in the moonlight. Harper hadn't been back since the accident, and in her imagination she'd pictured a burned strip of land strewn with torn metal and ash. But, aside from the small memorial, the spot looked no different from any other stretch along the road.

She sat down on the ground, tugging her sweater around herself, and waited. There was no reason to expect that he'd come. Even if he got her message, the odds were low that he'd bother to show up. Especially after the way she'd treated him these last few weeks.

But she was holding too much inside. If he didn't show, maybe she could just scream her pain into the night; maybe that would make everything somehow better. She stared at the thin, white wooden boards and wondered why she didn't cry. Being here should offer some kind of release, she thought in frustration. Instead, it just made her feel disconnected; it didn't seem like anything that had happened here could have any connection to her.

The road was empty, and when the headlights appeared on the horizon and drew closer, splashing her with light, she knew he'd come for her. The car pulled off the road and stopped. A door slammed, and footsteps approached.

"Okay, Grace. I'm here. Now what?"

Harper stood up to face Kane. The smirk dropped off his face. "What the hell is wrong?" he asked. "You look like shit."

"Gee, thanks."

"Seriously, Grace, what is it?"

"It's . . . everything." Harper rubbed her hand against the back of her neck, trying to ease the tight knots of muscle. "I just wanted to . . . I need . . . I—" She wanted to tell him everything: how she couldn't even remember what it felt like not to be miserable; how every night she went to sleep dreading the next morning; how she wanted to escape from inside her head and just become someone else, with a normal, happy, guilt-free life. But the words froze somewhere in her throat. "I'm sorry," she said, turning away from him. "I thought I could do this, but I can't." She shook her head. "Sorry I dragged you out here. You should just go."

"I don't think so." Kane grabbed her arm and spun her back around. "Talk to me, Grace. What do you need?"

"What the hell do you care?" she sneered, pulling her arm away.

"I'm beginning to wonder that myself," Kane said, arching an eyebrow, "if this is the thanks I get. . . ."

"Whatever." Harper walked away from him, wishing she

could just keep walking, into the darkness, and disappear.

"Hey!" Kane followed. *"Harper!"* he grabbed her again.

"Get off of me!"

"I'm not leaving you here alone!" he shouted.

Harper forced a laugh. "As if you care about anyone but yourself."

"Insult me all you want, but I'm not leaving."

She smacked his arm, then his chest. "*I* am."

But Kane threw his arms around her and pressed her fiercely against him.

"Let go of me!" she cried, banging her fists into his back. He ignored her and just held her tighter. "Kane, please! Please. Just let me go."

"And then what? You get to finally be alone? You think I don't know I'm your last stop?" He stopped shouting. "I'm not like the rest of them—you can't push me away. Come on, Grace, you know I always stick around until I get what I want."

She burst into laughter, letting herself sag against him, and in that moment of release, everything she'd been holding down so tightly came flooding to the surface, her laughter quickly turning into gasping, wracking sobs.

And Kane held her as she cried.

"This is natural," she hears the doctor say to her mother as she lies still in the bed, unwilling to move, or speak, or do anything but stare at the ceiling and wait for the nightmare to end. "She's in shock. Give her a chance to absorb things. It's all a part of grieving."

It doesn't feel like grieving. It feels like falling.

"I killed her!" Harper screamed, shaking. "I did it. She's dead. I did it." Tears gushed down her face and she gasped for breath, wishing she could just pass out so the pain would end.

"It was an accident." Kane insisted. "It *wasn't your fault.*"

But she wasn't listening. She was remembering.

They won't tell her what happened to Kaia. They won't tell her anything. Until, one day, when she is "strong enough," they do.

"Kaia didn't . . . didn't make it, hon. I'm so sorry."

Harper doesn't say anything. She doesn't feel anything— just . . . empty. It doesn't seem real. Things like this don't happen to people like her. She doesn't cry.

"It should have been me," she moaned.

"No."

"Yes."

"Harper, no."

The memories flowed faster, beating her back in time through the misery, through the pain.

Everything hurts.

"Where am I?" she asks. Her voice sounds like two pieces of metal scraping together.

"There was an accident," her mother says, hovering over her. "You and Kaia. . . . Do you remember what happened?"

She doesn't remember anything. She feels like the past doesn't exist, that there is only the present—pain and confusion.

It isn't the first thing she asks. But, eventually, it occurs to her: "How's Kaia?"

"It should have been me," she said, letting herself fall limp in his arms. If he hadn't been holding her up, she would have fallen.

"Stop."

"It should've," she insisted.

"It shouldn't have been anyone," Kane said softly, smoothing her hair down.

"I wish I could just go back." She closed her eyes and lay her head against his shoulder. It was wet with her tears.

"It's going to be okay, Grace."

The tires screech as she spins the wheel, but the car won't move fast enough. The van is bearing down, and next to her, Kaia screams and screams as the car shakes with a thunderous impact and rolls off the road. The world spins, Kaia screams, and everything goes dark.

Harper shuddered. "Nothing's ever going to be okay." But her sobs had quieted and she realized she could breathe again. She took a few deep breaths.

"Better?"

"Don't let go," she murmured. Not yet. She wasn't ready.

"Never," he promised.

The wind rushes past them, and Harper can feel everything fall away until nothing is left but a crisp, clear certainty that life is good, and that she is happy. Kaia turns the music up, and they shout the lyrics into the wind, their voices disappearing in the thunder of the engine.

She presses her foot down on the pedal. Faster, faster, the world speeds by, her life fades into the distance, she can leave it behind if she just goes fast enough and far enough.

"Let's never go back!" she shouts to Kaia.

"Never!" Kaia agrees, tossing her head back, laughing.

They have everything they need. A fast car. A sunny day. Freedom. Each other.

She has been so miserable, so angry, so afraid, for so long, and now all that has burned away, and there is only one thing left.

Joy.

Here's a taste of the next *sinful* read . . .

Gluttony

"Now *this* is more like it," Harper gushed as they turned onto the Strip. "Civilization. Thank god."

"Mmm hmmm."

"Okay, how much longer are you going to give me the silent treatment?" Harper asked, exasperated. "I already told you I was sorry. How was I supposed to know that you'd find—"

"Don't say it!" Miranda shrieked. "I'm trying to block it out of my mind forever."

"Okay, okay. How was I supposed to know you'd find that *thing* in the sink? I only volunteered to take the toilet because I thought it would be the easier job, and it is your birthday weekend, after all."

"Celebrate good times," Miranda deadpanned, and suddenly, in sync, they both burst into laughter. "Did all that really happen?" Miranda sputtered through her giggles. "Or was it just some mass hallucination?"

"I wasn't hallucinating the smell," Harper gasped, waving her hands under Miranda's nose. "I washed them ten times back there, and they *still* stink."

Miranda wiggled away, trying to focus on the road. "Don't even talk to me about smells," she groaned. "It'll just remind me of . . ."

"Don't even go there," Harper cautioned her. "You're just going to make us both sick."

"Again."

They shook with hysterical laughter, and Harper closed her eyes, soaking in the moment. It may have been the most disgusting night of her life, but things between the two of them were actually starting to feel back to normal. There was a time when Harper had feared they would never be close again; mostly because of the things she'd done and said, and all the things she couldn't bring herself to say. *I'm sorry. I need you.* But somehow, they'd found their way back to their bickering, bantering norm, and that meant that the long ride, the many detours, and the adventures in raw sewage had all been worth it.

Well, almost.

When they finally found the hotel, they pulled into the lot without registering much of the medieval tackiness of the garish white tower. It was nearly two in the morning, and they could only focus on two things: a hot shower and a soft bed. Both were now, finally, in reach.

They checked in, ignoring all the other Haven High seniors who littered the hallway—it seemed half the school had hit Vegas for the long weekend, and they were all staying at the Camelot, less for its bargain-basement prices than for its widely renowned attitude toward its underage denizens: Don't ask, don't tell.

Usually Harper would have lingered among the admiring crowd; she never let a moment in the spotlight go by without putting on a suitable show. But the fewer people who saw—and smelled—her in this state, the better. The girls trekked down a dingy hallway and arrived in front of room 57. Harper swung open the door to discover a small, squalid room with two full-sized beds and little else. Miranda immediately dropped down onto the one closest to the door, stretching her arms with a satisfied purr. "I could fall asleep right here, right now."

"Perfect, because I call the first shower," Harper said, dumping her bag and rushing to the bathroom before Miranda could object. She could feel the stink and filth crawling over her skin and needed to scrub it away before she could enjoy the fact that she was finally, after a lifetime of waiting, spending a weekend in Las Vegas.

And after nearly drowning in misery for three months, she planned to enjoy the moment as much as humanly possible.

She opened the door of the bathroom, stepped inside—and screamed.

Adam grabbed a towel and tried to cover himself, but it was too late. Harper had seen everything. Every tan, muscled, gleaming inch of him. She felt faint, and it was all she could do not to lunge across the bathroom and sweep him into her arms, perfect body and all. But she forced herself to stop and remember: she and Adam were no longer best friends, as they'd been for half their lives. They were no longer in love—*lovers*, she told herself, her mind lingering on the word—as they'd been for far too short a time. They were . . . nothing. And she intended to treat him as such.

"What the hell are you doing in our room?" she snapped, trying to regain her equilibrium. *Don't look at his chest*, she told herself. *Don't look at his shoulders. Don't look at his arms. Don't look* . . . This was maybe not the most effective strategy.

"*Your* room?" Adam tugged the towel tighter around himself and took a step forward, as if to escape the bathroom—which would mean his half-naked body brushing right past Harper's, a fact he seemed to realize just in time. He stopped moving, and Harper refused to allow herself a moment of disappointment. "This is *our* room. We checked in hours ago!"

"And 'we' would be . . . ?"

"Me. Kane. We. Our room."

And then it all made sense. From the sour look on Adam's face, Harper could tell he'd figured it out, too. "Very funny, Geary," she muttered to herself. "Very cute." When Kane had offered to pay for her and Miranda's room for the weekend, Harper had figured it was just an uncharacteristically gallant gesture, an extravagant birthday present for Miranda. (And not that extravagant: According to the website, rooms at the Camelot went for sixty dollars a night.) She should have known better.

"Harper, look," Adam began, "since you're here, maybe we can—"

"I'm out of here," Harper snapped. Adam refused to let it rest. He couldn't get that if he didn't want a relationship with her, she wasn't about to accept the consolation prize of his friendship. Not when she knew what he *really* thought of her. But he just wouldn't take no for an answer, and kept forcing her into these tedious states of the union talks without realizing the torture they inflicted on her. As if she didn't want him in her life, desperately. As if it didn't kill her to remember all the things he'd said when he'd broken her heart, how he hated her, how he could never trust her again, all because she'd made a few not-so-tiny mistakes. And then his belated and halfhearted offer of forgiveness, just because of the accident, just because she'd gotten hurt and Kaia had—

No. She'd resolved not to think about any of that this weekend. She was taking a vacation from her pain and her guilt and everything else that had been weighing her down. Kane *knew* that, and was still pulling this crap? Unacceptable.

Harper backed out of the bathroom and, without a word of explanation to Miranda—who was already half asleep—rushed out of the hotel room in search of her target.

"Harper, wait!" Adam called down the hallway. She glanced over her shoulder and, sure enough, he was standing in the hall wearing only a towel, flagging her down. She didn't stop—but grinned to herself when she realized that he'd let the door slam and lock behind him.

Just before reaching the elevator, she heard a loud thud and a shouted curse.

Sounded like he'd realized it, too.

Kane sighed, and reluctantly tore himself away from the stunning blondes to answer his ringing phone. He allowed Harper about thirty seconds of ranting before cutting her off. "I'll meet you in the lobby in five," he promised, snapping the phone shut again before she had a chance to respond. He had been expecting her irate call and, though the face-off could easily be avoided for hours, he preferred to get all potential interruptions out of the way now. The blondes could wait.

After all, this weekend was too important, and his plans

too delicate, to risk interference from a wild card like Harper. And from the sound of it, she was about to get pretty wild.

"What the hell were you thinking?" she raged, as soon as he came into sight.

"Nice to see you, too, Grace," Kane said dryly, spreading out on one of the Camelot's threadbare couches. (The pattern had likely once been intended to resemble a medieval tapestry, but now it just looked like Technicolor puke.) "Have a good drive?"

"Lovely, thanks for asking." As if the sarcasm had sapped all her energy, she sank into a chair beside him. "Seriously, Kane, what's the deal?"

"The deal with . . . ?"

"Adam? In *my* room? Taking a shower? Any of this ringing a bell?"

Kane smiled innocently. "Adam's up in *our* room—yours, mine, his. Ours. Think of it as one big happy family."

"And it didn't occur to you to mention that this was the plan?"

Kane shrugged. "Did you think I was going to pay for two hotel rooms? I'm not a bank, Grace."

"I—" Her mouth snapped shut, and he knew why. Given that he was footing the bill for the trip, it would be pretty tacky of her to complain about the lodgings. And Harper Grace was never tacky. "I just would have liked some advance notice, that's all," she said sullenly. "You didn't have to ambush me."

"If I'd told you ahead of time, you wouldn't have come," Kane pointed out. Adam and Harper had been on a monosyllabic basis for a month now, and Kane was getting sick of it. Not because he felt some Goody Two-shoes need to play peacemaker, he told himself. Just because there weren't too many people in whose presence he could tolerate; it was troublesome when they refused to share breathing room.

"What do you want me to do?" she asked, a hint of a whine entering her voice. "Make nice and pretend like nothing ever happened between us? Not gonna happen."

"That's not my problem, Grace," Kane told her. "Speak to him, don't speak to him, I don't care." Not much, at least. "But this is the only room you've got, so unless you don't plan on sleeping or bathing this weekend—and, no offense, but I think you're already overdue on the latter— you should probably get used to it."

"But—"

"Gotta go," he said quickly, bouncing off the couch. "Allie and Sallie are waiting for me in the casino. Twins, if you can believe it." He wiggled his eyebrows at her, and, miracle of miracles, she cracked a smile. "Now, your mission, and you have no choice but to accept it: Chill out, shower, and then grab Miranda and meet me down here in one hour. We're going out."

Harper checked her watch and rolled her eyes. "Geary, it's the middle of the night, and some of us have been on the road for an eternity."

Kane shook his head. "Grace, this is *Vegas*." Why was he the only person capable of understanding this concept? "Night doesn't exist here. It's a nonstop party, and we're already late."

"I don't know . . ."

"Since when does Harper Grace turn down a party?"

He knew perfectly well since when, and that was why he'd insisted she come this weekend, and why he'd dragged Adam along for the ride. Harper had been on the sidelines long enough—it was time for her to get back into the game. Whether she wanted to or not.

It was good pot—strong, smooth, decently pure—but not good enough to help Beth sleep through Fish and Hale's impromptu jam session. (Featuring Hale's off-key humming and Fish banging Beth's hairbrush against the wall for a drumbeat.) After an hour of tossing and turning, she'd finally given up on trying to sleep—only to discover that Reed was wide awake, lying on his side and staring at her.

"What?" she'd asked, giggling at the goofy expression on his face.

"Nothing." He'd given her a secretive smile, then a kiss. "Let's get out of here." And, still clad in her T-shirt and purple pajama shorts, she'd followed him out the door. They'd gone downstairs in search of the pool, running into half the Haven High senior class on their way.

Beth didn't care who saw her or how she looked. Only one person's opinion mattered to her these days, and only one person's presence made any difference.

Make that two.

Beth saw her first, and tried to dart down a hallway before they were spotted, but it was too late.

"Well, this is just great," Harper said, lightly smacking her forehead. "As if my weekend weren't perfect enough."

Just ignore her, Beth told herself. She couldn't afford to get into a fight with Harper—not only because she'd inevitably lose, but because she'd promised herself she would stop hating Harper. Yes, she'd done her best to ruin Beth's life—but Beth's attempt at revenge had nearly succeeded in ruining Harper, permanently. Just as she would always bear the guilt for Kaia's death—*don't think about that*, she reminded herself, as she constantly needed to in order to make it through the day—she would always know that Harper could have just as easily been the one who died. That *Harper* was the one who'd landed in the hospital, gone through painful rehabilitation, emerged pale, withdrawn, and the object of too much curiosity and not a little scorn. They were more than even, although Harper would never—*could* never—know it.

But forgiveness was easier said than done. And even the sight of Harper still made Beth's stomach twist.

"Hey, Harper," she said softly. Reed pressed a hand against her lower back, as if sensing she needed physical support to keep herself upright.

Harper's eyes skimmed over Beth without stopping and zeroed in on Reed. "Having fun with the new girl-friend?" she asked, disdain dripping from her voice. "Guess it's easy for some people to forget."

Harper tried to push past them, but Reed's arm darted out and grabbed on to her. *Just let it go*, Beth pleaded silently, wanting only for the moment to end quickly, without bloodshed. But she could tell from the look on his face and the tension in his body that he'd already been wounded.

"I haven't forgotten," he told Harper, in a low, dangerous voice. "Kaia would have—"

"Don't say her name," Harper ordered him, her voice

tight and her face strained. "Don't say anything. Just *enjoy* yourself. I'm so sure"—though it wouldn't have seemed possible, her tone grew even more sarcastic—"that's what *she* would have wanted."

A moment later, Harper was gone, and Reed was the one who needed support. But when Beth tried to touch him, he stepped away.

"I'm sorry," she said softly, knowing he wouldn't understand what she was apologizing for.

"It's not you." He wouldn't look at her. "It's nothing."

When they first met, he had talked about Kaia nonstop. But something had changed—Beth never knew what, and never wanted to ask. Reed had kissed her, and, after that, had never spoken of Kaia again. There were moments when his voice drifted off and his eyes stared at something very far away, and she knew then that he was wishing for something he couldn't have. But he never said it aloud, almost as if he had to force himself to forget Kaia, in order to allow himself to be with Beth.

Or maybe she was just projecting, because the only way she could be with Reed was to force herself to forget. Kaia had died because of her—no, phrasing it that way avoided the truth—she had *killed* Kaia. Accidentally, maybe, but killed nonetheless. And now, reluctantly, guiltily, but undeniably, Beth had taken her place.

She wrapped her fingers around Reed's, half fearing he would pull away. He didn't—but he still wouldn't meet her eyes. "Let's go find the pool," she murmured. He nodded, and she squeezed his hand. He felt so solid, and so safe. He wouldn't disappear, she reassured herself. He would never leave her alone.

Unless he found out the truth. Then he would be gone forever.

"Down to business," Kane said, rubbing his palms together in anticipation. "How should we kick things off? Blackjack? Poker?"

Miranda didn't want to admit that she didn't know how to play any of the standard casino games—though she had a vague idea, courtesy of *Ocean's 11*, that roulette wouldn't actually require anything other than choosing a color. She'd rented the DVD in anticipation of the big trip, but had been too distracted by George Clooney to glean much more information than that.

She also didn't want to admit that she would be happy enough to spend the whole weekend without coming face-to-face with a dealer, since surely they'd take one look at her height (or lack thereof) and sallow baby face, and show her the door. Or whatever it is they do in Vegas when they bust you for having a fake ID.

But she didn't want to seem timid or clueless, not in front of Kane—and especially not when he was giving her that lascivious, anything-goes smile—so she shut up.

Fortunately, Harper, who frequently argued that Kane looked more like an over-tanned weasel than he did a Greek god, didn't have any such qualms. "We're not in Loserville anymore, Geary," she reminded him, "and the bouncers here aren't blind. No one's going to believe we're twenty-one."

Kane shrugged. "Didn't have any trouble getting served earlier, did we, Morgan?"

Adam's face was a purplish shade of red. "Let's hit the slots," he said abruptly, turning away and stalking toward the dollar machines. The rest of the group followed behind, two-thirds confused and one-third triumphant.

"What's *that* about?" Miranda whispered to Harper.

"Don't know, don't care," she said shortly.

Harper had been in a pissy mood ever since the Adam encounter, and Miranda knew better than to press the issue. She was just feeling her way back to normal with her best friend, and Adam was too much of a hot-button topic to broach—at least at three in the morning. Besides, she was afraid that if they started talking about sharing a room with the guys, Harper might see through Miranda's commiseration act and realize the truth: she loved the idea. Sharing a room with Kane? Even if there were two beds and two other people, even if Vegas was filled with far flashier women to catch Kane's eye, even if it was almost a statistical impossibility that anything would happen, Miranda couldn't help but hope.

This was Vegas, after all, which meant that anything could happen . . . which meant that, despite the odds, something *might*.

All the action was happening over at the tables—the slots seemed the sole territory of the blue-haired old ladies and a few caved-in old men with bad toupees and giant plastic buckets, all waiting for their big payoffs. Miranda dug into her pocket and pulled out a fistful of quarters, plugging them into a rain forest–themed machine that touted itself as the "Green Monster." She put her hand on the long silver lever, then sucked in her breath as a warm, strong grip closed over hers.

"Feeling lucky, beautiful?" Kane murmured from behind her.

Miranda bit down on the corners of her mouth in a pointless attempt to suppress a smile. Was he, too, thinking about the last time they'd been in a casino together, the last time—the only time—they'd kissed?

Probably not. For Miranda, it had been the culmination of five years of hoping, dreaming, waiting; for Kane, she knew it had just been a fast way to liven up a slow afternoon.

Still, he was here, so close that she could feel his chest just grazing her back, and she knew that all she'd have to do was step backward, and she would be in his arms.

She stayed where she was, and pulled the lever.

Too late, Miranda thought, and she began to wonder: What if she hit the jackpot? If the movies were any guide—and really, if the movies *weren't* an accurate guide to life, she was totally screwed, since they were pretty much her sole source of information—sirens would blare. Coins would pour out. People would cheer and stare. And security guards would sweep her away before she could touch a dime.

There was no siren, no jackpot, no cash—and the man who lurched toward her, his breath reeking of gin and his meaty hands grabbing at her chest, was no security guard.

"You're a liar!" he slurred, his hand tightening around Miranda's shoulder as he staggered against her.

"Get the hell off," Kane snapped, shoving himself against the drunk, who squeezed even tighter, and who would have taken Miranda down with him as he stumbled to the floor, if Kane hadn't ripped her arm away. She shook him off, too, trying to catch her breath, telling herself that nothing had actually happened. No reason to panic, she was fine.

Too out of it to pull himself up, the guy writhed on his back like a crab, pointing at Miranda and howling. *"Liar!"* She couldn't look away. "You're all liars!"

"Can we get a little help here?" Kane called, waving down the swarm of security guards.

Miranda was dimly aware that Harper and Adam had joined her on either side, that Adam's hand was pressing down firmly, protectively on her shoulder—that she was shaking. But none of it really registered.

"It's all going to come out," the drunk moaned, as the guards hauled him off the floor. He pointed at Miranda, then Harper, then swung toward Kane. "There are no secrets," he hissed. "Not here." The guards grabbed his arms and began to drag him away, slicing through the crowd of gamblers and disappearing behind the glittering slot machines. A moment later, as his howling cries faded away, there was only giddy laughter, clanging machines, canned jazz, and the occasional hoot of victory. The normal sounds of Vegas—like nothing had ever happened.

"You all right?" they all asked Miranda, who nodded like it was.

She forced a smile. "What an asshole, right?"

Crisis averted, Kane's smirk reappeared. "But it's true, you know. About Vegas. This is where the secrets come out. Everyone here's a liar, but . . ." He narrowed his eyes and pursed his lips in an exaggerated scowl. "It takes a damn good liar to beat Vegas. This is the city of truth."

Adam dropped his hand from Miranda's shoulder and quickly stepped away, and she wondered whether he was thinking the same thing she was. Their secret—one drunken night together, a hookup she barely remembered, a memory they'd both agreed to forget, to bury forever—could ruin everything. And there was no reason for anyone to ever find out—no reason for *Harper* to find out.

Unless Kane was right. Unless there *was* something here, something in the air, in the oversized drinks or the adrenaline rush, something that forced secrets out into the light. . . . Miranda stole a glance at Harper, whose face was ghostly pale, her eyes darting back and forth between Miranda and Adam, her lip trembling.

And then Miranda had a horrible thought. She'd worried for weeks that Harper would find out what had happened, would misinterpret an innocent, unimportant, drunken mistake as something more than it was. Something unforgivable.

But what if all that worrying had been a waste—what if she already knew?

All she had wanted was an escape. A return to normalcy.

What an idiot.

Of course Kane was right, Harper thought, suppressing a moan. Of course this is where the secrets came out to play—everyone drunk all the time, never sleeping, pushing themselves to the limit, letting their guard down. It's a disaster waiting to happen.

It was *her* disaster. What if they found out somehow? The image forced itself back into her head, the one she'd been trying to forget—the one she'd driven hundreds of miles to escape. Her hands on the wheel, her foot on the gas pedal, the world spinning. The flames.

They all pitied her now, but if they found out she'd been the one behind the wheel, if *Adam* found out . . .

She told herself she didn't care what he thought, not anymore. But she knew he could never forgive her for being a murderer. Why should he? It's not like she had found a way to forgive herself.

Two days, she thought. *Forty-eight hours.* If she could survive the weekend, stay sane, stay hidden, keep the real her—the unforgivable her—under wraps for the weekend, it would be a sign. She had hoped for a vacation from the torment of her life, but maybe that's not what she needed. Maybe she needed one final test, proof that she could put the past behind her and focus on normal life, that she could live with keeping quiet, that she could go on, even here. She would survive Vegas, and that would be proof—she could survive anything.

"Forget the drama, guys," Kane said, drawing the group toward the exit. "We're wasting valuable party time."

"I'm, uh, thinking I might get some sleep," Miranda said, staring at the ground.

"Yeah." Adam's gaze was fixed on the ceiling.

"Maybe they're right, Kane—" Harper began.

"What the hell is this?" He pointed ahead of them to the giant neon sign blinking a few feet away: MIDNIGHT MAGIC BUFFET—24-HOUR FEAST. "It's two-for-one drinks tonight. What are we waiting for?"

"No more drinking tonight," Adam said. "Not for me."

Kane gaped at the three of them as if they'd sprouted antennae. Then a look of understanding spread across his face. "I get it." He nodded, and grinned. "I spooked you. Look. I'm sure none of us have any secrets. . . ."

He turned to Harper, who met his stare without

flinching. He knew what she had to lose—and she knew he was daring her to chicken out.

"But let's just say, hypothetically, we all do," he continued. "So I suggest a pact. We'll drink to it. Anything we find out about each other this weekend . . . well, it doesn't count. All secrets forgotten as soon as we leave the city limits. After all, what happens in Vegas—"

"I don't drink to lines that are so old they have mold growing on them," Harper snapped.

"What happens in Vegas, *stays* in Vegas," Kane finished, arching an eyebrow. "Agreed?"

They nodded, and they shook on it. Not that it mattered. Harper knew she was the only one with a secret that really meant something—and there was no way in hell she was risking exposure. Pact or no pact.

"Good. Let's get ourselves some cocktails and make it official," he ordered, charging toward the buffet. "Eat, drink, and be merry, for tomorrow—we do it all over again."

about the author

Robin Wasserman enjoys writing about high school—but wakes up every day grateful that she doesn't have to relive it. She recently abandoned the beaches and boulevards of Los Angeles for the chilly embrace of the East Coast, as all that sun and fun gave her too little to complain about. She now lives and writes in New York City, which she claims to love for its vibrant culture and intellectual life. In reality, she doesn't make it to museums nearly enough, and actually just loves the city for its pizza, its shopping, and the fact that at 3 a.m. you can always get anything you need—and you can get it delivered.

You can find out more about what she thinks of New York, L.A., books, shopping, pizza, life, the universe, and everything else at www.robinwasserman.com.